THORN OF
DARKNESS

Also by: Katie Richard

Destiny Of Graystone Series:
Destiny
Into The Storm
Thorn Of Darkness
The Rise Of Chaos
The Duchess Of Destruction
The Shadow Realm

Standalone:
My Last Hope

The Frayed Outlaws Series:
More Than Our Fake Vows
Falling For The Drummer

THORN OF
DARKNESS

KATIE RICHARD

CONTENTS

CHAPTER 1

Sierra

The off-white walls of this tiny office feel like they're closing in on me. The only sounds are our collective breaths and the clock's incessant ticking on the wall.

Tick, tick, tick.

With each passing second, my future with the Guardian Academy is on the line. Dread builds in my stomach like a brick, heavier and heavier, waiting on what my punishment will be for using my gift against Adeline and her clique of bitches.

Watching them knock Emma's books to the floor as they slammed her against the lockers made me unbelievably angry. But, knowing Emma was hiding how bad it was getting? That hurt like hell. Why would she hide that from me? After everything we've been through together. She's my best friend.

Sweat beads on my upper lip. God, it's stifling in here.

"Three-day suspension," Headmaster Matias says deadpan. His receding hairline is even more pronounced underneath the fluorescent lighting. His black-rimmed glasses slid to the base of his nose while he studied me like a bug under a magnifying glass just minutes ago.

"What? No. You can't do that!" My voice is on the edge of hysteria as I begin to stand. The chair screeches as the legs scrape on the linoleum.

I've worked far too hard for them to do this to me. It's not fair. After everything I've sacrificed for Graystone.

"I just did." His lips form a tight line.

"But-"

"Sierra! Calm down," Uncle Joe growls while glaring at me and pointing his index finger at my chair.

I hastily lower myself back down and cross my arms over my chest to keep myself rooted to the spot. Everything in me wants to fight this. It's not right. Emma has the right to her education without being harassed.

Matias assesses my barely contained rage. "Whatever you have to say for yourself, Ms. Walker, it's too late. You knew the rules on using magic against another student, or *students* in your case."

"As I said, they were bullying Emma," I say through gritted teeth. "Four guardians in training against a half-breed, come on, how the hell can you justify their actions? Are they even getting suspended?" I lean back in my chair as my foot taps out the beat of my frustrations. My body nearly hums in agitation.

"Their punishments are none of your concern. The academy will not tolerate bullying and is looking into the accusations." Matias places his black and gold fountain pen on top of the closed notebook on his large desk.

"Yeah, I bet," I mumble, shaking my head as my eyes are drawn to the grains in the cherrywood desk.

I highly doubt the four golden girls will get in any trouble. It doesn't help my case that Adeline's dad is on the school board and is a major benefactor. I found out that little tidbit after confessing to Dante what had happened. If those four knit-wits even get detention, it'll be a miracle. Without me here, who will make sure Emma's safe? I can't get suspended. Emma needs me.

"Ms. Walker, since you like to add things in when they're not needed, how would you like to make it a longer-term, hmm? Seven days? Ten? Or how about expulsion?" his booming voice echoes off the walls.

Matias's beady eyes stare into mine, begging me to back-talk him again. I bet he's enjoying this. The headmaster never seemed to like me anyway. He's always staring me down and barking orders at me. I clench my jaw to keep myself from lashing out. The fury builds inside me, coiling and coiling into a tight knot within my stomach.

"Sir, may I speak?" Audrey asks him.

I almost forgot she was also in this office, which smells like dirty old feet. The humid air makes the scent even more repulsive. Audrey teaches many of the guardian classes here at the academy and has been supportive of my unusual arrangement here. She's the only instructor who offered to come to my aid today. The rest couldn't be bothered.

"You may." He leans back in his leather chair, creaking the fabric under his bulky weight.

"I just wanted to say that Sierra really is a bright young woman with an amazing amount of potential in her." She glances at me with a warm smile. "I know her intent wasn't to harm those girls but to protect the weak who can't protect themselves, and that is the meaning of an immortal guardian, is it not?"

"Your point?" Matias taps his fingers on his desk, clearly irritated.

"I personally haven't witnessed Emma being bullied, but I have seen Adeline harass Sierra in my classes. I'm not saying the other girls deserved what's being insinuated, but how far can you keep pushing somebody who's been through so much trauma in such a short while without thinking they'll snap under the pressure?"

I gaze down at the floor, willing the tears away that form in my eyes at the mention of my *trauma*, the battle that led to my mother's death. Great, now I'm just a traumatized guardian in training. That's exactly what I want them to think of me, not. Everybody in this country has known loss in some way.

"What are you suggesting?" He tilts his head to the side, focusing his attention on her.

My pulse thumps in my chest like a jackhammer. My palms sweat. I could lose everything because of what I did. Audrey takes a deep breath, and her gaze is unwavering on me as she speaks to him.

"After the three-day suspension, I'll take Sierra under my wing. I'll ensure she has a safe outlet for her aggressions and coach her through this to become the guardian I know she can be."

I offer her a grateful nod as the headmaster sighs and rubs his chin while staring out the window. His silence stretches on as my heart continues to thud hard in my chest. Waiting on his verdict is agony. It's like waiting for the guillotine to either fall or spare you. His decision could go either way. In this moment, he holds all the power. I hate that fact. I loathe the feeling of not being in control.

He sighs before answering, "Okay, but on one condition."

I exhale the breath I held in a rush. Oh boy, here we go. What does he want me to do now?

"When you arrive at school, you'll wear these daily, no exceptions." He reaches into his desk drawer and pulls out a pair of silver bracelets. "You break my rules, and you'll be expelled. Are we understood?" He raises his eyebrows.

Great, now I get to wear iron handcuffs all day. I sigh in defeat. It's better than getting kicked out, and at least they're coated with silver to look like a regular bracelet. But, I'm sure everyone here will know exactly what they're meant for, to snuff my gift out. I won't be able to use my hydrokinesis while wearing these. Iron is the only thing powerful enough to strip any immortal of their gifts, even the most vile of them all, Excalibur.

"I understand, sir. Thank you," I say quietly, reaching for the metal bracelets.

I stand to leave, but he clears his throat, drawing my attention over my shoulder. I just want to get out of this room. This morning's already drained all my energy.

"One more thing, Sierra." Now the other shoe's going to drop. "I'm aware of what you had to do and sacrifice to protect our people. Graystone will forever be indebted to you for that."

I swallow thickly and look away as the wetness coats my eyes again. It seems they're always so close to the surface lately. As if my infinity for water is what rests just below my skin.

"Whether you know it or not, I'm just doing my job as headmaster to protect all the students here. I'm not trying to be uncaring to your situation, but your gift is powerful and uncontrolled, and I have to take these measures to ensure everyone's safety."

"I know." I nod, hating that he makes a valid point.

My gift is powerful and terrifying to many, sometimes even myself. I raise my chin back up before walking out into the empty hallway. I won't show anybody weakness. I was weak once before, and look at the damage that caused. I'm not that girl anymore; I've changed in so many ways.

Audrey and Uncle Joe follow me out, their shoes tapping quietly behind me. She wraps me in a hug and tells me it'll be okay. Not Uncle Joe, though. His judgment of me is clear. He's angry and disappointed in me. Would my mom be disappointed in me as well?

I only have to struggle with that debate for a mere second. She wouldn't be. Mom would be proud that I stood up for Emma and protected the weaker being. After all, she was a guardian long ago.

"I'll walk you to your dorm room and let you grab your things," Audrey says, leading the way.

"Wait, what? I can't even stay in the dorms?" That leaves Emma completely exposed at all times.

"I'm afraid not, Sierra. Anytime somebody's suspended, they're not allowed on the academy's grounds."

"What about Em-"

Audrey rests a hand on my shoulder. "I already took care of that. Jack will walk with her from class to class and back to the dorm to ensure she arrives safely."

She knew I'd get suspended, that or suspected it. At least she thought ahead for Emma's sake. I'm grateful that at least one adult in this hallway has my back. If I'm getting kicked out of here for a few days, I think I want to go to the beach.

Wait, maybe not. I almost forgot about what happened during my last beach trip. The Scylla that attacked Dante and me is dead, but who's to say there aren't more of them waiting to strike? I shudder at the memory. Yet another thing ruined for me.

Maybe I'll return to the Caribbean castle and finally get to snuggle up and read from that massive library. Dante's working the rest of the week but can always portal to wherever I am. I don't say goodbye to Uncle Joe as I turn and start walking down the long corridor. All he's done is treat me like a child since the spat in the hallway was reported.

"You can do better than this, Sierra," his voice trails after me.

I stop abruptly and twist on the heel of my sneaker. "Are you serious? Hold the lecture, please," I snap. "There's plenty you could've done better too. Maybe if my entire family hadn't lied to me since birth, *I* would've been better prepared for this shit storm." I throw my hands up in the air.

I'm still angry that they hid everything from me. I hate that I'm mad at my mom as well. It's hard enough to deal with her loss, but how can I get closure when I'll never know the answers to most of the questions plaguing me late at night?

"That's different, and you know it," he replies, scrubbing a hand through his short beard and sighing.

Why does he think he can be the only one who makes decisions for others' well-being? I shake my head. "Yeah, you're right. It is different. I hurt four girls that were assaulting and harassing my best friend. But you? I don't even know who the hell you are anymore." I twist on my heel and cast one more glance at him over my shoulder.

"Sierra-"

"Goodbye, Uncle Joe." I cut him off and continue down the hallway.

Since we sent my dad to that treatment facility, Uncle Joe thinks he can take his place and try to boss me around. News flash, buddy, you're not my dad, and even if you were, I'm an adult. I can answer for myself. I know I shouldn't have used my gift on them. I guess I'll have to work that much harder to excel in combat training and beat them that way. Wouldn't that be something, them losing to the newbie?

New life goal. Fight like there's nothing left to save. In the end, there may not be anything left, anyway.

Eric

Standing in the alleyway beside Ruby's apartment, my nerves are high. I've been planning this night for a while. Nervousness thrums in my veins and makes my mouth go dry. I've always had a way with the ladies. Unfortunately, it seems that Ruby's immune to my charms. I steel myself for her possible rejection.

"Do you trust me?" I ask Ruby, pulling a blindfold from my back pocket.

"No," she scoffs, giving me a clear, you must be entirely out of your damn mind look. Her large brown eyes widen when they land on the soft red scrap of fabric in my hand.

I can't say I didn't see that answer coming. Unfortunately, knowing it was going to happen didn't lessen the sting. My lips tighten into a firm line to prevent the hurt from showing on my face.

"I won't do anything to hurt you," I tell her softly, shaking my head as I step closer.

Ruby takes a tentative step back. Her booted foot scrapes on the pavement. "I'm pretty sure that's what all the serial killers say as they lure unsuspecting girls to their doom." She places her hands on the gentle curve of her hips.

I tilt my head to the side and study her. "So now I'm a serial killer?"

This woman and all her wild ideas. She has a child's imagination but a woman's snarky attitude. An older man with gray hair walks by the alley's opening and stares at us. His dark eyes bore into me as he gauges the scene before him. Giving him a pointed look to move along, he finally gets the hint and scurries away. Thanks to Raymond, not many people like to associate themselves with me. But tonight, it works in my favor.

"Are you?" She shifts her weight from one foot to the other. Her eyebrows draw down, and wrinkles form on her forehead.

I bite back the laugh that threatens to come out. "I'm not."

"Why do you need the blindfold, then?" Her eyes narrow at the offending red satin blindfold.

"It's a surprise." I flash her a grin, hoping my anxiousness isn't showing through.

I can't screw this up. I don't know what it is about her, but I need to be near her. When we're apart, those chocolate-colored eyes haunt my dreams.

"I don't like surprises," she stammers, twisting the black and red ring on her finger. It's one of those anxiety rings that's meant to glide across one another to calm the wearer. One of my exes wore one.

No shit. "You told me the other day you needed more than what being a guardian can provide. It's too calm for you. This is me offering a way for that to happen."

"By abducting me? I don't know what kind of *thing* you're into, but I'm not game for that." Her hands fling around in the air as she talks.

I move like a flash of lightning. Bracketing her between my arms against the brick wall, she has nowhere to go. Her mouth falls open in a surprised gasp. Her soft, floral-like scent swirls around my brain, making concentrating hard. I'm no saint, but what she implied straight up pisses me off.

Once her gaze finds mine, I lean down, my breath kissing the shell of her ear, and I tell her, "Unwilling participants isn't my *thing* either." She sucks a haggard breath in. "When we're together, it'll be because you want me just as much as I want you. Now put the damn blindfold on," I growl the last sentence, half in anger and half in a desperate attempt to hold back from kissing her.

Ruby gulps in the air like she can't get enough. Her chest rises and falls rapidly, coming mere centimeters from my own. Every nerve ending where our bodies nearly touch is on fire.

I slowly pull away from her but never take my eyes off hers. I've never had to chase a woman this hard in my life, but I know I'm wearing her down at a fucking snail's pace. We'll get there. I know we will. I just need to keep chipping away at the armor that protects her like a shield.

She snatches the silky soft garment from my hand with a huff. "Fine."

Tugging the elastic across the back of her head, I take in her rigid posture, standing with her hands fisted at her sides. Ruby breathes in through her nose and blows out past her lips. I don't know what's happened to her in the past to make her this way, but obviously, whoever did it took her feeling of safety away. They made her into this powerful but scared female whose only weapon is to push men away.

That ends now with me.

"I'm making a portal, and then I'll guide you through it, okay?" I tried to suppress my anger at her situation and my building tension and keep it out of my voice, but it sounded harsh to my ears.

"To where?" she squeaks. Her fisted hands open and close a few times.

"Adrenaline."

Her lips narrow into a frown as the portal morphs our landscape into a swirling cloud of smoke. A gray metal storage facility surrounded by trees comes into view.

I place a hand on her lower back to gently push Ruby toward the opening, and her muscles tense beneath my palm.

The temperature is milder here in Colorado Springs than it was back in Graystone. The sliver of the moon is the only light in the back corner of the grounds, and the crickets chirping loudly in the distance disappear into silence. They know when predators are nearby.

"Can I look yet?" she snaps impatiently.

"Not yet." I chuckle under my breath.

Flipping the key back and forth between my thumb and pointer, I decide to make it fast. Ruby's cooperating, and I don't want to push my luck. I got her farther than I thought I would already tonight. I didn't think I'd even get her to put on the blindfold, let alone dutifully follow me. Now for the moment of truth.

As I unlock the door and roll it up, I glance over my shoulder. Ruby slowly turns her head from side to side as if she can figure out where we are by the sounds. The motion light I installed roars to life with a flicker. I swallow thickly. I'd never brought anyone here before; this was my sanctuary.

My black and chrome Indian cruiser stands proudly in the center of the small space, with a small workbench and tool chest to the right. On the left sits a futon that was once comfortable but has long since lost its plushness, a small mini fridge, and a few boxes. A home away from home.

"Take it off," I direct her.

Without hesitation, she yanks the blindfold off as soon as the words leave my mouth. Her eyebrows scrunch together. "A motorcycle?"

I can't read the emotion on her face; she just went pale. There's no snarkiness or attitude, just nothing.

"Have you ever ridden one before?" I ask.

The muscles flex in her jaw as she swallows. "Never, you?"

"I've ridden for a few years." Stalking closer to the bike, I trail my fingers up the smooth black paint. I rest my palm on the custom artwork on the side of the gas tank. The gray smoke detail resembles shadows of people. Nobody knows about this, not even Emma. She'd kill me if she ever found out. Emma hates motorcycles. "Her name's Shadow Chaser."

"You named your motorcycle?" Ruby smirks.

I shrug. "That's my pride and joy."

That I share with no one. The only time I've ever felt free from the burdens my father placed on me was when I'd ride. It's just something about the open road, the wind on your face, and a beast below you.

Ruby turns slightly as if to sit on the futon but freezes when she notices what's draped over the side. "What are we doing here, Eric?" Her shoulders slump, and exhaustion riddles her features.

Gesturing to the bike, I say as if it wasn't obvious, "I'm gonna bring you for a ride."

Her eyes narrow. "Is this what you do with all the ladies? Take them out on your big bad motorcycle and woo them?" Her angry tone confuses me.

I thought she'd like this. She loves danger, and anyway she can get a thrill, she does. I mean, the woman chases down dark ones for a living. Motorcycles are like an adrenaline junky's wet dream. The way you can test the laws and physics of gravity is astonishing. A few times during my first days of riding, I was surprised I walked away. That kind of power demands respect. I've rebuilt this bike so many times I could take her apart and put her back together with my eyes closed.

"No woman has ever been on my bike. You'd be the first." Removing my hand from the tank, I stride closer to Ruby, unsure if I made a mistake springing this on her. I'm beginning to think I should've slowly broached the subject.

"Then what do you call these?" She picks up the matte black helmet and the leather coat I had custom-tailored for her. As the fabric shifts, she catches a glimpse of the back of the jacket. A large patch sewn into it shows a skeleton hand holding a black rose, wearing a ruby on the ring finger. Her mouth opens and closes twice before she whispers, "What is this?"

I throw her a lazy grin as my chest swells. My confidence comes back, knowing I made the infamous rambler nearly speechless.

"Yours."

That one word holds all the power to make or break this night. The jacket is the only thing that can even remotely come close to what she means to me. I've never done anything like this for anyone. I never felt the need to, but with Ruby? It's just the tip of the iceberg. I rub my palm against my breastbone in an effort to massage away the ache that's been a constant for a while.

"These haven't been on another broad's body?" she asks, her gaze never leaving the jacket in her hand. Her eyes trace the pattern repeatedly as if the woven threads could spill any dirty secrets of mine.

"Nope," I make a popping sound with the p. "Brand new."

"Why me?" She still won't look away from the garment.

This is a question I've asked myself. There's just something about Ruby that draws me in. "I wanted to give you a piece of me that nobody else has had," I pause. "Something just for us."

Ruby sucks her bottom lip into her mouth. Reaching a hand up, I gently grab her chin and loosen her red-stained pouty lip with my thumb. Her eyes finally meet mine, and there's a sheen of tears coating them. I don't think she's ever allowed a man close enough to care for her the right way.

"Go for a ride with me?" I ask quietly, my thumb lightly caressing the side of her jaw.

Her only answer is a nod. Taking the jacket out of her hands, I open it up and hold it out for her to slide into. Twisting around as she zips it up, it's a perfect fit. Slim at the waist and broader around her chest. The gemstone on the patch nearly matches the same red shade of her hair. Damn, she looks fantastic in leather.

I've thought of this moment a hundred times. Only I thought it would be Sierra standing beside me. Taking a deep breath, I admit it still hurts deep in my soul that she'll never be mine. Maybe she was never meant to be. Ruby could be the one I was meant for all along. We both have a tragic past, but I don't know what hers is yet.

I will find out. When I do? I'll do everything I can to make the hurt fade.

CHAPTER 2

Ruby

Pulling the helmet over my head, I try to hide my shaking hands. I struggle three times to latch the strap under my chin and fail with an exasperated sigh. Eric clasps my fingers in his, and my breath stalls in my chest. Those deep sapphire eyes hold mine captive.

My heart's beating erratically in my chest. The panic attack sits there just on the edge, threatening to take over my body as it has before. The walls close in on me, nearly choking the breath from my throat.

"Hey, we don't have to do this if you're uncomfortable," Eric's calming voice reaches through the fog in my brain.

I am uncomfortable, but how can I tell him why? How could I tarnish his meaningful gesture? I can't tell him how just seeing a motorcycle, no matter the difference in appearance, brings me back to a tormented childhood. I came to dread hearing the loud exhaust of Brooks's bike coming down the road.

That's the thing with abuse; you may grow beyond it, but you'll never be free of it. There are still parts of my life that continue to haunt me, jagged edges that poke through when you least expect it to.

I'm not sure I'll ever be ready to open that wound with Eric. The only men aware of what I went through are Mav and Alex. I don't want Eric to see me as that damaged little girl afraid of the world. I want him to see me for who I am today, the woman I've grown into.

As I'm lost in the sea of blue, the skin around his eyes crinkle. I suck in one last slow breath as my pulse slows to almost normal. The loud beating in my ears is now only an echo. His inky black hair is longer than when I saw him last. The ends touching the top of his brows. His lips tilt up in a reassuring smile as my will to say no withers away.

"But I want to," I tell him honestly. I need to do this. It's another trigger I need to obliterate into nothingness. Something that shouldn't still have a grasp on my life.

"Okay."

Eric releases my hand and clasps the strap together. His warm fingers lightly graze my chin as he tightens it until the nylon rests against my skin. Eric nods and steps away from me.

He pushes the motorcycle out of the storage unit, and I follow him outside before he secures the door. Throwing his plain leather jacket on with a matching helmet, he swings a leg over the intimidating heap of metal. Grabbing his shoulders for balance, I hop on behind him, thankful I'm wearing skinny jeans today instead of the plaid skirt I almost chose. I'm sure the first gust of wind would show all the goods to everybody on the street. Not that anybody's around. The night is silent save for us, and the light rustle of wind that shakes the trees.

Eric reaches forward with his arms, and a loud rumble makes me jump. My pulse hammers so hard it feels like I may pass out. It's okay. It's just a pedal bike with a motor, and it's Eric. I'm safe.

Wow, I never thought I'd say that. Safe with Eric? I swallow the bile that threatens to come up. What the heck did I get myself into now?

Placing a firm hand on my thigh, he leans back into me and turns his head. "Are you sure?"

I can't see his whole face, only the tension that wrinkles the skin around his eyes. The dark blue hue of his irises are like sapphires in a sea of onyx. I nod, not trusting any sound I make to be louder than the beast purring beneath me.

"I'll go slow at first. If you need me to stop at any time, pinch me, and I'll pull over right off."

"Alright," I squeak. God, I sound like such a girly girl. This is not who I am. I don't show fear to anyone, especially men.

"Hold on tight." Eric grabs both of my hands and tugs them around his rock-hard abdomen, pressing me flush against his back.

His dark, musky scent, tinged with the fragrances of the ocean, sandalwood, and eucalyptus, nearly overwhelms my senses. Eric slaps the kickstand back with his foot and balances the machine on his powerful legs for a minute before twisting the handlebar and making Shadow Chaser come alive. As he pulls away from the building, some tension releases from my shoulder blades. I'm really doing this.

The wind whips my face once he turns onto the pavement and picks up speed. He maneuvers around corners seamlessly as if the rugged wheels are an extension of himself. With every slight movement he makes, the muscles ripple under my arms. The power that lurks beneath his skin, being able to command this giant death trap, is close to melting my panties right off. I never thought of myself as a motorcycle chick but with him? Maybe. But let's not tell him that.

The city skyline off in the distance glows on the horizon. After riding silently and tucking my face into Eric's back at times when things seemed to blur by too quickly, my blood is still pounding. It's not a pulse-pounding terror but like a rush of giddiness consuming me. When Eric pulls the throttle harder, the force pulls me back slightly. I tighten my grip as a squeal sneaks past my lips.

"Faster!" I shout over the deep grumble of the bike and the wind rushing in my ears. The force of the wind threatens to throw me off.

I don't hear his laughter, but I feel it quake through his back muscles just before he punches it. The wind pulls at me. My thighs clench around his, and I squeeze him so hard with my arms that I'm surprised he can still breathe. If it bothers him, he doesn't show it. I hold on tight and let the road draw my laughter out. I haven't felt this free in... as long as I can remember. It's like the whole world drifts away, and it's just us under a clear, star-flecked sky.

We drive around mindlessly, weaving in and out of towns with no destination in mind. The night air soon turns to a biting chill. My torso's well protected by Eric's body and my beautiful new jacket, but my legs are freezing. Either feeling my shivers or knowing my bottom would be getting sore, Eric takes us back to his makeshift garage. Or is it a man cave? He-shed?

Once I get off, he pushes Shadow Chaser back in her spot and gestures for me to sit on the futon. Eric pulls the overhead down but leaves a gap at the bottom, keeping most of the draft out. Gingerly sitting down as the soreness seems to seep farther and farther into my muscles, I watch as Eric pulls over a patio heater and snags a navy blanket from under his tool bench. I wonder to myself if he stays here frequently. A sharp pang hits me in the chest. It seems his life is just as lonely as my own.

"Want a beer?"

"Sure," I answer, watching him turn away with a newfound appreciation for the man he is.

He's not just some frat boy with a pretty face. I was too quick to judge him. There's a lot more to him than I ever thought possible, and I get the feeling I've barely scratched the surface.

Reaching into the compact fridge next to me and grabbing two bottles, he settles beside me and spreads the blanket over our laps. There's about a foot of space between us, but I can still feel what it was like to be pressed against him. The warmth that radiated off his skin and through the fabric where our bodies touched left a tingling reminder.

"What'd you think?"

"It was amazing!" I beam at him. I don't feel the invisible cage's iron bars around me for once. "Thank you."

He takes a sip of his drink. "Glad to hear it. You're welcome." A grin nearly splits his face in two. His pearly whites are sparkling in the low lighting.

The pull to want to kiss him is strong. It must be the adrenaline wearing off. I never feel a fluttering sensation around men—certainly not ones like Eric. Bad boys like him are only good for a fun night, nothing more. He makes me want more, though. That scares the crap out of me. I never want more with anybody. I know he had a thing for Sierra; you can see it in his eyes when she's within his sight.

I don't want someone who's pining after another girl. I've lived far too long to play those mind games. When I decide to have a relationship with a man, he has to be all in.

Dante

I feel ridiculous. I hate doing undercover ops like this. I'm dressed like a spoiled twenty-something partier. My jeans are the only normal thing. The dressy gray button-down I wear must be left open at the top. According to Maverick, "The ladies love it like that." I tug at the collar.

I had to leave my katana at home, only bringing a few daggers with me. I can shield them from view to humans, but not vampires. I feel naked without the weight across my back. The loud music thumps through the open doorway, where a hefty bouncer is busy carding people. A team of six of us is coming in tonight, but we're staggering our entry times to hide our intent. We've received reports that the owners host illegal feeding parties for vampires in the back.

I try not to take on extra cases like this, where I could be gone for days at a time. Even if Sierra can't come home during the week, I still like to be close if she needs me. The High Council couldn't assemble a strong enough team on such short notice, and Burkly City falls in my jurisdiction, making me better equipped for the job.

I've never been a big fan of nightclubs, all those sweaty bodies crammed together along with a thick layer of drugs pumping through the human's blood. This place reeks of bad decisions.

The bouncer steps in our way and raises his hand. "IDs," he bellows in a deep voice.

He's a few inches shy of my six feet. At this height, you can see the thinning of his dark hair on the top of his head. Reaching into my back pocket, I pull out the fake ID I use while in human territory. Maverick follows suit. The wide-set shoulders of the bouncer taper down to a broad chest and torso. To other humans, he'd be intimidating; no doubt that's the look they're going for. His brown eyes match our faces to the little pieces of plastic, and he nods for us to pass.

Walking in, we squeeze through the crowd and spot a pair of open bar stools in the corner. That would be a great spot to keep an eye on things. I tilt my head in that direction and sigh when several women try to run their hands down my chest and pull me onto the dance floor. "Maybe later," I tell them as I shake them off.

A persistent tiny blonde tugs on my arm again. The pungent smell of alcohol permeates my nostrils, and I fight the urge to wrinkle my nose in disgust while I twist out of her grasp. I glimpse small white scars lining her neck as she turns back to her friends. Vampire bites. It looks like we're in the right place.

Finally reaching the bar, we settle in and order some nachos and a beer. We can't be too conspicuous while we scope out the place. I lean toward Mav. "Did you see the blonde?"

"Yep. Looks like she's a feeder."

The others arrive soon after, announcing their arrival through the small, nearly invisible earpieces we're wearing. A few vampires mingle in the crowd before disappearing down a long corridor. I'm keeping tabs on one particular vampire, the owner. His dirty blonde hair is styled, and he grins every time he sips off the black glass from which he's drinking. I'd wager it's not just alcohol inside it.

Francis dons slacks and a light blue Oxford, but he scans the crowd as if looking for somebody. This is the part I hate: waiting for something to happen. Patience is something that's drilled into us at a young age, but I've always found it difficult to stand by and wait.

A handful of humans walk down the hall as well, and only a few have come back out. That leads me to believe there are more than just bathrooms back there. That must be where they have the entrance to the feeding rooms. The owner waves a hand to a tall, lanky man who just came through the doors and heads toward that dark corridor.

"I'm gonna go take a leak," I tell Maverick, but also speak into the earpiece. My team knows that's the code for checking around.

I casually glance around as I stalk through the crowd. When I round the corner, the restroom signs are lit up in neon green but that's not what snags my attention. An armed guard is standing in front of thick, red velvety curtains. Now, why would you need a guard here?

I walk closer, but he barks, "You can't come through here."

"Why not?"

"Private party." He swings open his suit jacket as if I couldn't see the barrel of the gun poking out through the bottom.

Staring into his eyes and focusing my mind, I command him, "I'm invited, and you'll let me pass."

His eyes don't dilate and take on that far-away look they usually do when we use our compulsion on humans. His hand reaches for the gun at his waist, and I dart behind him and wrap my forearm around his throat, cutting off his air supply. He struggles in my arms, trying to pry my grip from him, but it's no use. I'm too strong for him. I flex the muscles in my arm as he swings at me. Once he stills, I drag him into the men's room and heft him up on the toilet. Locking the stall door and portaling on the other side, I tell my team we're a go. That should buy us some time.

I smooth down the wrinkles in my shirt as I step out into the dimly lit hall. "Ready?" I ask.

Tugging the curtain back, they rush through. Only one dark red door remains at the end. Landon kicks the door in, and the team of guardians storm inside. Half-naked women lay atop stone slabs as multiple vampires feast on their flesh. Small glittering chandeliers above each table bask them in an unforgiving light. The humans are unusually pale and riddled with bite marks. The air is cooler back here as if all the air conditioning is channeled into this one room. More like a morgue than the backroom of a bar. A shiver creeps up my spine.

Chaos ensues as the vampires yell and run in the opposite direction to another door. As it's yanked open, soft light filters through. There must be another exit into the parking lot that wasn't on the blueprints.

"Landon!" I shout above the shrieking of the women left bloodied on the table. The vampires never sealed the dripping wounds before taking off. They took off and left them to bleed out.

"On it," he replies as he runs out the door behind the escapee.

The rest of the team is subduing three other vampires, and Marissa is tending to the two humans' bite wounds. She tears open a bag of clotting agent with her teeth and packs the small leaking holes.

I snake my arm out and grasp the shirt of a male trying to escape. He swings his elbow back and lands a hard blow to my ribs, knocking the wind out of me. Thrusting him to the stone slab the victim lies on, I shove his head down, bashing his face into the cold stone. Blood trickles down the smooth surface. A strangled yelp comes from him, but he still tries to break free of my hold.

"If you'd stop fighting me, it wouldn't be this bad," I snarl.

With a knee pressed firmly between his shoulder blades, I pin him in place while grabbing the cuffs from my back pocket. I slap one on the wrist I'm already holding and reach for his free hand.

"Screw you." He slams his head back and into my chin, pinching my lip between my teeth.

"Shit." A coppery taste fills my mouth, but I don't release my grip on him.

I clench my other fist and drive it into his side. He drops to the slab as a gargled puff of air releases from his body. Wrenching his arm behind him, I quickly place the cuff on and lock it as tight as it'll go. Then, for good measure, I push it harder until an extra click snaps into place.

"Stand up," I bark at him.

Struggling to pull his legs under him, I yank hard on the chain connecting the iron handcuffs until he's upright and still heaving in oxygen.

"Marissa, status?"

"They lost a lot of blood, but they'll be okay. The ambulances are on their way."

Landon comes back empty-handed. Running his hand through his short hair, he meets my gaze. "He got away."

"Continue to stake this place out in case he comes back," I instruct.

"Will do."

Marissa stays behind, ensuring the humans receive treatment, leaving the four of us with a prisoner each. Transporting them through a portal to the Guard proves to be the simplest task of the night. After dumping the vampires in a cell and filing the necessary paperwork, I bump into Nilo on my way out of the building.

"I really think you should put eyes on the six keys," I tell Nilo.

We call the group that performs the ritual that keeps Excalibur locked away in his prison deep inside Mount Olympus the keys. It's a fitting title, considering only they have the power to imprison him or set him free. Nilo is also one of them.

"I don't think that's necessary, and it may draw more attention to them than if we didn't." He tucks his hands into the pockets of his slacks. The master council doesn't wear his traditional robing unless he's in the High Council building. A stark difference from the prior leadership.

"I'm telling you, something's not right. It's too quiet. The dark ones are plotting something. I can feel it." It's like an unsettling mess of snakes in my stomach. Every time something feels off, they slither around more. I shudder. Snakes repulse me even more since the battle with the Scylla.

Nilo twists his lips around as if hesitating to reply but doesn't drop eye contact. "You may be overreacting with your need to protect your bonded mate."

My jaw clenches painfully. Yes, I'm protective of Sierra, but this is more. "My gut hasn't steered me wrong before. It's a mistake not to have protection on them. Don't they deserve that after everything they have to do?" I bite out. They're the ones who have to maintain the spell monthly and deal with the evilest immortal there is, Excalibur.

"I understand your wariness, Dante. But nobody has knowledge of our roles besides the ones who were there." His lips tilt up at the edge as if to convince me all is well.

"Anybody could've seen us all leave together and put the pieces together. They could all be targets. You're underestimating Excalibur's followers." If it's any indication from the number of traitors at his compound when we stormed it, there's more out there.

Our conversation drops off as an immortal enforcer swings open the large iron doors. "Gentleman," he greets us before taking the stairs two at a time and banging a right around the next building.

"Your concerns are noted, and if there's any evidence that they're in danger, I'll assign a protection detail to all of them. Myself included."

"Thank you." I know I won't get anywhere with him right now.

I hope they never find themselves in danger, but others will notice a pattern as time goes on. The same people disappear every full moon. Our training hones in on patterns and little things that others may not notice. I'm sure there are still traitors hiding in plain sight.

The cell phone in my pocket vibrates, and Nilo takes the opportunity to disappear beyond the doors of the Guard. Sliding it out, I grin when I notice it's Sierra's name on the screen.

Her text reads, "I'm suspended for three days. I'll be in the Caribbean."

I shake my shoulders, trying to release some of the tension. I had a feeling this would be the outcome. She knows the rules, and she broke them. Her punishment is more lenient than I thought it would be. Headmaster Matias isn't known for showing mercy with his discipline.

"I'm sorry, beautiful. I'll see you soon," I text her back.

I knew her meeting would be held this morning. Maybe that's what's been messing with me today. Excalibur won't settle for being confined in that jail cell. He's biding his time. You don't build an army as he has and then just lay belly up like a submissive dog.

He's got a plan. The only way out of that mountain is if somebody collects all six of the ritual stones and performs a spell. As long as each key has the gem in their possession, he can't leave. That's the only knowledge that lets me sleep easier at night without Sierra in my bed.

Creating a portal to the castle, I'm rewarded with the sight of Sierra doing laps around the makeshift track with just a pair of shorts and a sports bra. Tied up high in a ponytail, her long brown hair whips behind her in the wind. And here I thought

I'd find her moping around about the incident's conclusion at the school. I should've known better. She's a fighter.

Her black sneakers smack against the dirt as she powers through another two laps before noticing me and jogging over. Pulling her earbuds out but not pausing the rock music pouring out of the speakers, she says, "I didn't think you'd be home this early."

The sunlight glistens on the small beads of sweat that formed at her hairline. I take her wrist in my hand and tug her into me until her body is pressed against mine. Then, she rests her head against my shoulder. Her anger comes through our bond, but there's also sadness. There's been sadness ever since that battle in India.

"I worked the late shift last night." I kiss her forehead. "I'm sorry that you got suspended."

"Me too. But it was worth it. Hopefully, they'll get the hint to leave Emma alone." Her lips twist before settling into a frown.

"I hope so, too. But there's other ways you can handle those situations."

She pulls away slightly to look up at me. Her arms are still wrapped around my waist, but a coldness seeps in from the loss of her warmth. "I know. Hold the lecture, though, please. Uncle Joe already tried."

"I wasn't going to lecture you. You know it was wrong. I'm asking what I can do to help. Whatever you need, I'm here."

"I need to get better at hand-to-hand. That way, I can kick their asses the good ole fashion way." Sierra smiles sweetly. "No special gifts needed."

A chuckle escapes from my chest. "There's my girl. You wanna practice with me?" I wiggle my eyebrows at her suggestively.

Her beautiful hazel eyes twinkle with mischief. "Always."

"I'll go get changed." I make a show of devouring her with my eyes. My gaze sweeps from her long tan legs over her toned stomach and full chest, finally resting on those hazel eyes that trap me in their depths. "You should stay in those, though."

Her grin widens. "Oh yeah?"

"Yeah," I answer as I turn away and jog to the castle to dress in clothes that will be more comfortable to spar in. I'm still wearing the clothes from the club, and it's hot as the fifth circle of hell here today.

Throwing on a set of gym shorts and a t-shirt, I make my way back out into the scorching sunshine. I find Sierra resting in the shade of the mango tree. Hearing my footsteps, she stands, and we begin to spar.

As our feet dance on the grass, she swipes a right hook at my chest, but I grasp her fist in my palm as I gently kick her side. Practice or not, I can't hit her like I do the others I spar with. She lets out a huff.

"Come on, Dante!"

CHAPTER 3

Sierra

He's holding back. I sigh loudly. My irritation is made very clear.

"I don't want to hurt you," Dante says.

I rub at my temples, trying to clear the chronic headache. The crappy sleep I've been getting is taking its toll on me, and I'm trying my best not to get snippy with him.

"How am I supposed to get better at this if you won't fight me for real?"

"It's different for bonded males. We're hard-wired to protect our females at all costs. Physically hurting you is damn near impossible for me." He swings his fist a little too far to the right and misses my face easily.

"So what you're saying is I need to find another male guardian to spar with?" Righting my footing, I swipe my right foot toward his stomach, but he catches it in his grip.

I try to pull my foot back, but he has an iron grasp on my ankle. Dante's grip tightens to near painful. His eyes narrow, and a low growl comes from his lips. "If you want him to suffer my wrath, then by all means, go ahead and find another male."

Oh, my flipping god!

"Seriously?" I yank my foot harder, and he finally releases it. Stumbling backward to right my footing, I mumble, "Don't be a jackass."

His eyes darken, and he lunges for me. Before I know it, I'm airborne. Thunk. My body falls hard to the ground, and pain lances through my back and radiates out through my extremities. The breath knocks from my lungs in a whoosh. Quicker than I can blink, Dante's covering my entire body. The grass is cool against my sweaty skin as his weight presses me down. His gorgeous face hovers just above mine.

"It's not something I can help, Sierra. You're my anima gemelli. The thought of another man putting his hands on you? Hurting you?" He pauses and places a kiss on the vein pulsing hard in my neck. "I see red. I could barely contain it when we were training here together, and those were my friends. I can't be held liable for my actions if another man touches what's mine."

"Then be who I need you to be and train me to fight harder." I sigh as a frown forms my lips into a line. "I need this, Dante. I can't let them win." I fight the quiver that threatens to show the emotion in my voice. I refuse to be weak.

"I'll try." He rolls off from me and holds a hand down to help me up.

Taking it, he pulls me up, and we go at it again. In dodging Dante's advance, I lost my footing and tripped over my damn foot. I'm not as good with footwork as others in my classes. Jumping up, I place a jab in his side, and he winces slightly.

Dante squares his shoulders and tilts his head to each side, eliciting a soft crack. Just standing there in front of me, he's like a wall of muscle, primed and waiting. Slowing my breaths down, I wait for his next move. I've seen him during practice and against actual enemies. He's patient and calculating, watching every inch of my movement like the dangerous predator he is.

I'm light on my feet as I fake a swing to his left, but ultimately, my fist swings hard and takes him in the right pec, making his steps falter slightly. I lunge behind him as he swings in retaliation. He's still holding back as he twists and lands a kick to my thigh. The force sends me stumbling before I right my footing.

Shit. Easy or not, that one hurt. I hold my arms up in front of my chest, waiting for his advance, but nothing comes. He smirks at me when I meet his gaze, knowing I have very little patience. Narrowing my eyes at him only makes his grin wider.

"Is there a problem?" he goads.

"Nope. Not at all." I smile sweetly at him as I land a hard kick to his stomach, making the air rush out of his lungs in a huff.

Stepping to the side, I jump on his back and wrap my arms tightly around his neck and head as my thighs squeeze his middle like a vice. The low rumble of his laughter makes me giggle and slightly loosens my grip. I yelp as he drops his knees to the ground, jostling me around before laying back and squishing me into the dirt and grass with his back to my chest.

"Get off me, you big brute." I squirm below him, trying desperately to shove him off.

Dante turns and begins tickling my sides as I grumble out the words, begging him to stop. By the time he stops, I can barely breathe from laughing so hard. Tears streak down my cheeks, and he gently brushes them away before collapsing on the ground beside me.

I needed this, just him and I. A sense of peace I don't usually have envelopes me like a soft cloud. We lie there on the grass for what seems like hours until the stars twinkle above us. Snuggling tighter against his side, a low rumble of thunder sounds in the distance. A flash of pink jets across the sky, illuminating the trees and wall that line the property. A slight sprinkle falls all around us and rests on our exposed skin like dewdrops.

I've always loved thunderstorms—the natural ones, that is. Mine are great, too, but with these ones, I can relax and take it all in, enjoying the beauty of Mother Nature. Another flash lights up the sky.

"Do you think they can see us from up there?" I whisper. "From the afterlife?"

"I like to think so. Growing up in Graystone as a child, we were told stories of the afterlife." Dante points up to the sky. "Each star is one of our loved ones that passed on. During the clearest nights when the clouds are nearly non-existent, the veil between the living and non-living is the thinnest. The firelights that shine when the sky is the darkest and hardest to see through are the strongest. The ancient ones are still tasked with watching over us even from beyond the realm of the living. Their duty never ends."

A thick lump forms in my throat as a hot tear cascades down the side of my face. "I wish it wasn't so far away."

His hand slides across the top of mine until our fingers are clasped together. "Me too. But, think of the ethereal view they must have up there. The sunrises and sunsets against the backdrop of all of us down here? We'll see them again when it's our time. For now, we need to live the lives we were destined for."

A bright light streaks across the sky as a loud crack of thunder follows in its wake. The rain turns heavier as the sky lets out its own tears. Droplets fall down all around us and on us.

"And what is that exactly? The lives we're destined for?" I ask.

"We each have our own task that the ancestors chose for us, but how we deliver it is up to us."

My throat tightens, only letting small puffs of air in and out. "And if we don't succeed?"

"Then we die trying," Dante says softly.

"What if I don't want to be the Immortal Savior anymore? What if I can't do it?"

Dante turns his body toward mine, and I do the same. He reaches his hand out and slides his knuckles down the edge of my hairline from my eye and down to my chin.

"Being the Immortal Savior is in you. It's a part of you that can't be removed even if you try. Our destinies are wound within the fibers of our being, just like our bond."

It is she that is destined to be the Immortal Savior. The maker of rain who calls on dark skies will extinguish the flames he has brought forth to scorch the Earth to ash.

The words from the prophecy ring like an echo in my head. I extinguished his flames; he's imprisoned.

"But if we already defeated him, and I completed the prophecy, why does it feel like it's not over yet?"

Dante inhales deeply before replying, "Because I don't think it's over. He may be locked away, but that doesn't mean there won't be another person to take his place. Our duty to protect this world never ceases because somebody will always want to commit vile acts."

I sigh, trailing my fingertips down his arm from his shoulder to his wrists, stopping now and then to trace tiny hearts on his skin. The rain begins to puddle in the low spots of the lawn.

Dante stands and holds his hand palm up for me to grasp. A yearning look crosses his face, and my gaze is drawn to his sharp jawline and up to his lips.

"Can I have this dance?" he asks.

"In the rain?" I laugh as my own palm glides against his, and he yanks me up against him.

He grins that lopsided smile that makes my knees weak. "Why not? Are you afraid of getting wet?"

"Never." I trail my arms around his neck and stare into the dark abyss of his emerald eyes. Water falls from his dark hair as he tucks a wet lock of hair behind my ear.

Rain glitters down in the moonlight as he wraps his arms around me and begins to sway from side to side. Wetness seeps through our clothing and sticks to our skin. Dante kisses me softly on the lips before resting his chin on the crown of my head. The thunder is still serenading us with the music of my soul.

"We're in this together, you and I. You're the savior, and I'm your light. You run, I'll follow. You fall, I'll catch you. You rest, I'll watch over you." He swallows. "You fight,

I'll be your weapon. You are both my weakness and my greatest strength. We will weather every storm just like this." His arms tighten around me, pressing me even closer to him.

"I love you," I whisper against his throat. I don't know what else to say. I'm not poetic like him, but I say the only thing I can think of, "You're the flame of the sea. On the darkest nights, my soul will always follow you. No matter how dire the storm."

Ruby

"I wish you'd reconsider," Nilo comments.

He's not getting the hint. I exhale a long, drawn-out sigh. "You know where I stand on this. I hate the secrets the High Council keeps from its people."

"Some intel is best left confidential. For instance, we wouldn't want our special friend's location out there for the world to know, right?"

I roll my eyes and throw my head back against the couch. "Obviously, not everything needs to be public knowledge." Feeling restless, I stand and begin to pace the small living room. My bare feet slap against the narrow hardwood slats.

"I'm not just asking you to come back. I want you to be the captain and lead the team. We need somebody like you who'll fight for the right reasons. You're not afraid to say no to the jobs that don't align with the new Graystone. And you sure as hell know how to boss others around." He chuckles.

I huff a laugh at the last part. I can be pretty bossy when I need to be. He's piqued my interest. "What do you mean by saying no and a new Graystone?"

"If you don't feel comfortable with a job, you can turn it down."

I pause my footsteps. Huh, that's a new twist. Anything the High Council previously assigned us needed to be executed no matter what, at any cost.

"Really?"

"Yes. I'm trying to bring Graystone into a new era. A change is long overdue. It'd be a big pay increase, and you'd get to help form this government into what it should've been from the start."

I don't really need more money, but who would say no to that? Making a difference in how our country runs sounds like a lot of responsibility. But if I could steer it away from the crooked crap we've done? I can make sure we're not hiding things from our citizens that we shouldn't be. A knock sounds at the door. Strange, I'm not expecting anybody.

I bite my lip in thought. "Can I get back to you with my answer?"

"Yes. Of course," Nilo replies.

After ending the call, I toss my cell phone on the counter and look through the peephole. Ugh. It's Eric. I'm not in the mood for an emotionally damaged man today … even if he's sexy as sin. My own baggage is enough for me at the moment. Knowing I can't just leave him outside my apartment, I begrudgingly open the door.

"What's up, ghost boy?"

He smirks at me. "Not Casper anymore?"

The similarities between him and that sweet little ghost end with his ability to disappear. I grin back. "You're not exactly a friendly little ghost, are you?"

"I can be friendly." He wiggles his eyebrows suggestively, and I groan in response, making him laugh.

He struts past me, and I'm left still holding onto the metal handle with the door hanging open. I huff out a breath and shut it.

"What are you doing, Eric?" I ask him as he makes himself at home by grabbing a beer out of the six-pack he puts in my fridge and plopping on my couch. Still reeling from that phone call, my tone comes out a little bitchy.

It doesn't help that his presence puts me on edge. I still remember what it felt like to be on the back of his motorcycle the other night. Unfortunately, my mind likes to replay that moment whenever I close my eyes.

"We both had the day off, and I figured we could hang. But it seems somebody's moody today." He sets the beer down on the coaster and rubs his hand across the back of his neck. The motion makes his bicep bulge and stretches the fabric of the dark gray henley he's wearing.

My mouth waters and I quickly snatch my gaze from his arm. Men don't usually fluster me like this, I'm Ruby freaking Hart, and I eat guys like him for breakfast. Yes, I get the irony of my two names and hate it. That's why most people don't know my last name. But the ones that do? They don't question if I have a squishy red heart filled with romantic niceties. I'm a love 'em and leave 'em kind of chick. There are no flowers and chocolates on my radar.

I cringe inwardly as the guilt creeps in. "I didn't mean to sound bitchy. Just got off a strange call."

"Do you want to talk about it?" Eric leans back on the sofa, giving me his full attention. He actually seems invested in my dilemma.

Shrugging, I reply, "Sorry, I can't. Confidential." You know, the usual crap that comes along with Graystone. An audible sigh escapes me.

He takes a long pull off his IPA before setting the bottle on the table beside him. "It always is, isn't it?" Eric scrubs his palms over his dark blue jeans.

Trying to shrug off his comment all but solidifies my answer to Nilo. I hate hiding things from people I care about- record scratch. No. I do not care about Eric or how he looks at me like he can see through my defenses. Or the way I've seen other women practically throw themselves at his feet, but I seem to be the only one to hold his attention. Nope, I don't care.

Walking to the fridge to clear the dumpster fire raging in my brain, I grab a cold, pale ale and call out to him, "If I had a way to change the secrecy part of my job, do you think I should?"

He's quiet for a moment until I return and sit at the farthest end of the couch- away from him. I don't trust myself to sit too close. I always try to put as much space as I can between us. Hell, if it weren't rude, I'd pull a chair from the kitchen so I didn't have to feel the couch dip as he twists his muscular body in my direction. I won't think about those muscles. I won't. Okay, maybe for just a second. He does fill out that shirt nicely. And the way they moved and flexed under my hands when I rode his motorcycle—pure freaking ecstasy. I've gone far too long without a man.

"That depends. Do you mean with the people here in Graystone or humans all over the world?"

Oh. I didn't think about that. "I'd start here and see how that goes."

He stretches his arm across the top of the couch, and it almost reaches my shoulder, which is pressed into the leather. My heart does a weird flip inside my chest. It's almost like I want to feel his fingers brush against the bare skin my tank top fails to cover. I don't. Something's changed in me since he brought me on Shadow Chaser, and I'm undecided on whether I like the shift or not. My pulse races just beneath my skin.

"I'm no expert here, but I know the toll it's taken on me having to hide that much of my life from my friends and Emma. If I didn't have to hide who I was? I wouldn't." He takes another swig of his beer, his dark blue eyes never leaving mine.

I feel stuck, not being able to pull my gaze from his. I haven't even taken a sip of my drink yet, and it feels like I'm buzzing. When his eyes dance across my body and land on where there's the least amount of distance between us, my shoulder and his fingers, my body heats. He licks his lips, fueling the inferno raging inside me.

"What if I were to kiss you right now? Would you let me?" his voice drops seductively low.

My breath hitches. "And if I say no?"

"Then I wouldn't." He gives me a small, sad smile.

Time stretches out as I debate my answer. My body wants to, but not my mind. That horrible organ in my chest thrashes wildly at the thought of him kissing me.

His eyes soften, and his shoulders sag slightly. "Why can't you let me in?" he asks quietly, taking my hesitation for a no. I didn't say no.

"Because it hurts too much to let any man in," I breathe out the words in a whisper. The truth is painful, but it's who I am. I'm not used to this whole spending time with a man thing besides Alex. It's usually just a quick thing. Wam, bam, thank you, ma'am style.

"Ruby," he sets his bottle down on the wooden table before us before continuing, "I can tell you've been hurt. I'm not blind, but I need you to know I have no intention of hurting you."

"That's what they all said," I scoff. I've heard too many variations of that sentence from one too many men in my life. They've all been a steaming pile of lies.

He rises up on his knees and spears his fingers through my short red hair, holding my face inches away from his. My lungs cease to move. "They were dumbasses."

His eyes flick down to my parted lips. Before I'm aware of my actions, I tilt my head, rise up, and seal my mouth over his. He tenses momentarily before opening his lips and letting my tongue inside. A strange mix of feelings bubbles up inside me the longer we kiss. A five-alarm alert blares inside my head, but my heart begs me to throw caution to the wind and let this one in. He feels... right, even though he tastes like a hoppy orange. His dark musk wraps around my senses and pulls me in even deeper until all I know is him.

I pull back slightly and bite my lip. He takes the cue and settles back but sits closer to me. Not close enough that we're touching, but close enough that if I wanted to lean my head against his shoulder, I could. Something draws me to Eric, wanting me to close the gap between us. I want to be able to let go of all the bricks that line my heart,

but I can't. What's left of my bruised and battered heart can't take another beating.

A ringtone breaks his gaze away as he reaches into the front pocket of his pants. He

doesn't miss a beat. His eyes lock on mine again as he brings the phone to his ear.

"Yeah?" he answers in a gruff tone.

"Eric, they spray-painted our front door. "Emma's voice comes through the speak-

er. Immortals have good hearing, even if he weren't this close to me.

He closes his eyes and clenches his jaw before replying, "What does it say this

time?"

This time? That means this isn't the first time somebody's done this to his apart-

ment. Rage builds within me, and I must not hide it well because Eric throws me a

knowing grin. How can he smile at a time like this? Somebody defaced his property.

Again.

"It says Satan's children need to go home."

He shakes his head and rolls his eyes. "Creative. Stay inside. I'll be there soon." He

presses the end-call button. Then, to me he says, "I'm sorry, I have to go."

I nod, not sure what to say. He leans in and gives me a chaste kiss, the feel of his

lips lingering on mine after he pulls away.

He looks at me with a longing expression. "I'll see you later, Ruby."

"Do you need help?" I ask, not wanting him to have to face this alone. It's not fair

for them to judge him based on his father.

His eyes brighten. "I don't need help, but I wouldn't say no to the company if you

want to come."

"Sure." I try to calm my racing heart as I stand and avoid eye contact.

I've never been kissed like that before. I mean, there's always the little butterflies

you get with something new, but this was an all-consuming feeling of falling. All the

more reason not to let him do it again. Although I initiated the kiss, not him, the little

voice in my head balks at me.

I follow him into the portal, not looking at how good his ass looks in that dark denim. Emma will be there. We won't be alone. I won't kiss him again.

"I know Eric's gone a lot, and I'd feel better if you weren't home alone so much," Maverick says from Eric and Emma's apartment as the portal closes behind us.

"What about me?" Eric's tone doesn't sound too happy at the suggestion.

"Hi, Ruby," Emma says.

"Hey, Em." I wave my hand and smile at her. I've always liked Emma. She's a little sweetheart.

"I was just telling Emma, I think it would be a good idea for her to stay with me until this blows over."

"You don't think I can protect my sister?" Eric scowls and crosses his arms.

Oh boy. This isn't good. Far too many red flags are being thrown all around at the moment for me to comprehend how this went from zero to sixty so fast. My gaze meets Emma's. No doubt she sees the dick-measuring contest that's sure to go down between these two.

"That's not what I'm saying at all." Maverick releases Emma and puts his hands up. "They know where you live, and she's home alone a lot of nights and weekends."

"You work a lot, too," Eric barks and raises his eyebrows as if to challenge Maverick's statement while moving in his direction.

"Mostly during the day, but they don't know where my place is. And furthermore, they know not to fuck with what's mine," Mavericks growls the word mine.

"Do I get a say in any of this?" Emma pipes up, her face turning red. Her light blonde hair only makes the red stand out more.

Eric pinches the bridge of his nose and closes his eyes tightly. "He's right, Emma." He sighs. "You'd be better off staying with him for now."

Emma glances at me, and I shrug. No camaraderie among women on this. I think the men make a valid point.

"Fine. I guess I need to pack my stuff then," she says, nearly stomping down the hall.

Needing to escape the tension, I trudge through and grab a rag with a bowl of water. Maybe the door isn't the only thing that needs attention.

CHAPTER 4

Excalibur

I pace back and forth in the small confines of my cell. The patter of my bare feet echoes against the iron floor below me. It's the only sound I've heard for the past several hours. I've built up an immunity to the metal that weakens many other beings, and I allowed the enforcers to believe the iron chains that wound around my body on the way to this prison affected me. I barely noticed the metal's weak hold on my body.

The cold, damp mountain they have me tucked deep inside will only hold me for so long. I'll find a way to break that spell and escape from here one way or another. I only came willingly to ensure Rosalee would survive.

Everybody makes me out to be the villain, and most times, that doesn't bother me. But now? I wish everyone would realize everything I've done is to save our species from the destructive tendencies of humans. It takes a hard ass like me to be able to do what's necessary for our survival.

I wish Sierra would've joined me willingly. We could have been a force to be reckoned with. If I could've absorbed her power like I have many others, nobody could stop me from bringing freedom to all immortals and dark ones.

Why should we have to hide in the shadows, always catering to the needs of the feeble-bodied mortals? Hiding away because humans can't handle the truth that there's something out there superior to them.

I snort; the low sound fills the small space. I will have my revenge on those mere humans.

Prior to my imprisonment, with the help of Maggie, I was able to get my hands on some of the blood bags that were stored at the castle Sierra and her team called home. I usually need more blood to absorb another being's gift than what was supplied to me. Luckily, Raymond was able to replicate all the genes and markers of each bag and made several synthetic blends. Unfortunately, the bags were only labeled by blood type when they arrived. It would've been much easier if they listed whose blood it came from. Not all immortals have gifts, and not all gifts suit my needs.

Dante's, however, will work perfectly now that I'm trapped in this cell.

I haven't mastered how to manipulate all the aspects of a dream yet, but my ability to mind control helps to mask what I can't accomplish. I've practiced on a few trustworthy allies. Some of those are hidden amongst Graystone. Only about half of my army was in India at the time of the attack. I never have all of my allies in one place; that's just asking for trouble.

Searching through the dream realm is like a galaxy full of stars that burn bright and call out to you. Every one of them is desperate for an escape from their pitiful reality. There she is—my powerful little dewdrop. I latch onto the thread of her subconscious and pull her into me.

Sierra blinks rapidly in the bright light and shields her face with her forearm before looking around the cream-white room I made her think we're in. Her eyes land on me and instantly narrow into slits.

"You." Sierra points a finger at me. "Where am I? How are you doing this?"

Ignoring her questions with a smirk, I say, "I'm glad to see you too."

"You ruined my life." She swallows thickly as her nostrils flare.

I tsk. "No, my dear. You did. You chose wrong. You could've joined me without all the dramatics and made this much easier on yourself." And I'd still be able to have

Rosalee by my side if it wasn't for Sierra's team showing up unannounced at my compound.

I hid it from everyone that I had an anima gemelli. I couldn't show one single person my weakness. In the end, it still cost me the battle. I knew it was over when Dante raised his blade to her throat. I lost. Had Rosalee not announced our bond moments before, I believe I would have died at the hands of this untrained, scared young woman who stands before me now. Sierra doesn't realize the power she can wield with her gift. She doesn't yet know that together, we can bring the world to its knees. We can make all the mortals quake with fear at the mere thought of us.

"I'll never join you," she snarls.

She's a firecracker, just like her mother was. It's a pity Sophia had to die. I could've used her too. I step toward Sierra, and she backs up against the wall behind her, trying to escape me. The walls are barren, with no pictures or furniture in sight. There's not even a window or door. There's nowhere she can run to get away. Nothing she can use as a weapon against me.

"Are you afraid of me, little dewdrop?" I cock my head to the side, noting the fast pace of her breathing. A vein pulses hard in her throat.

Her nostrils flare again as her jaw clenches. "Don't call me that."

I go to reach for her, and she instinctively twists her hands as if she could produce magic to use against me. Her lips form a scowl when she realizes it won't work in here. She tries to sidestep me, but I cage her in with my arms against the wall, my face inches from hers. Her eyes dart from wall to wall, no doubt looking for an escape she won't find. I wait until she looks me in the eyes again before proceeding.

"I will get out of here, and when I do, I'm coming for you. Willing or not, you'll help me to usurp the humans." Holding her gaze, I try to reach out with my compulsion, but it seems she's immune to having her mind controlled that easily. That's okay; there are other ways to get what I want.

"Not a chance," she scoffs. "What do you have against the humans anyway? They can't do anything to you."

The humans may not terrorize me as they did in my early years before I'd learned my abilities, but I refuse to allow that to happen to another young immortal or dark one. I shudder to recall the atrocities and tests they performed on me. The secret world government faction, the Chemists, is comprised of the human world's leading scientists. They're the ones who take control of anything that goes bump in the night.

They're also the reason I have this ugly, jagged scar across the left side of my face. My body is how humans found out that iron can harm us. They sliced my cheek open repeatedly, watching as it kept healing itself. But each time my skin regenerated, the scar was larger and more pronounced.

"So young and naive. Humans are the reason we can't live our lives freely. They destroy what they can't control, and I'm done with staying in the shadows. I'm finished watching this world revolve around them. It's time for us to take our rightful place at the top. I'm offering you a partnership here. You'd be wise to take it."

"I'll die before anybody lets you out. I'll fight until there's nothing left of me but a pile of ashes." Sierra squares her shoulders and raises her chin, still several inches shorter than I. Her bravery is astonishing. Misplaced but impressive nonetheless.

"You brave, stupid girl." I shake my head. "I hope it doesn't come to that, but I have a feeling you'll come around." A slow smile twists my mouth as the plan formulates in my brain. She won't even see it coming.

My brother, Nilo, isn't the only one with a soul seer in his pocket. I know what I need to do. I'm good at figuring out what motivates people and manipulating them to fit my needs best. You just have to offer them what they want most in this world. And I know just the right proverbial carrot to dangle before Sierra. She'll mold to my whims like putty.

She doesn't reply. Sierra keeps glaring at me. She's a fighter; I'll give her that.

"Forget about all of this," I say and twist my hand, making the dream realm disappear in a cloud of smoke. I'm once again in my despicable temporary home, where the damp air seeps into my skin and bones like an eternal coldness.

One thing I've noticed with using compulsion on other immortals is that there's always a kernel left of what you made them forget. While she won't remember me coming to her in a dream because of the memory spell that was used, she may recall a part of our conversation. If I keep coming to her in her sleep and toying with her mind, she could go mad, and that is what I'm counting on. The less control she has over her own mind, the easier it'll be to use her for my benefit. To mold her into the immortal I need her to be. My little puppet.

There's a darkness in her. I can feel it even in the dream realm. It calls out to mine, begging me to set it free. That's exactly what I intend to do. Sierra's so caught up in doing what she thinks is right that she won't notice me chipping away at what keeps the darkness locked away on the inside. That thin, frail shell of righteousness will crumble under my skill until the darker parts of her can shine like that damn black obsidian stone she wears around her neck like a trophy.

We'll see who ends up with all the stones in the end.

Emma

It's been a week since I moved into Maverick's apartment. It's clear he may suffer from OCD with the way he organizes everything in his place. And I mean *everything*. Not only are his clothes separated by type, but they also go by a color flow. Short sleeve to long sleeve, light to dark. His closet is like a high-end boutique.

The towels in the bathroom are all folded the exact same way as well. The satin edges are all to the right and stacked in neat, identical piles. Everything about this place is orderly.

Maverick's taking me on a date tonight, and I feel nervous. We've been on several dates, but it seems different now that we live together. He works so much that I barely see him. I double-checked my hair and makeup for the final time before we headed out. I've never felt the need to impress somebody as much as I do him. I've been slowly falling for him ever since our first meeting.

Walking across the cobblestone driveway, he leads me to a small ice cream shop. The metal table and chairs are crisp white with bubble gum pink accents, making me feel like I'm entering one of my favorite childhood movies.

"Two root beer floats, please," Maverick tells the cashier.

"Coming right up," he chirps.

Once paid and drinks in hand, we sit outside at a table next to the front window. Other citizens of Graystone walk by the shop, either on a mission to the other stores or ready for the nightlife this part of the city boasts on a Saturday night.

Live music flares anytime somebody opens the door to a pub down the road, and soft, warm light shines down from the lamp posts that dot along the walkways. It looks like an adorable coastal town you'd see in a magazine. I haven't been here long but don't want to leave. There's something about Graystone that makes me feel like it's where I belong. It's the home I never knew.

With Maverick watching me from across the small table, I take a sip of my drink through the thick plastic straw. I've never had a root beer float like this. It tastes like a hot summer day. With notes of root beer, cream soda, vanilla bean ice cream, and something else I can't place. Caramel maybe?

"This is my favorite." He holds up the glass to the street light, and it twinkles a brownish gold in the rays. "Out of all the food and drinks that Graystone has to offer, nothing compares to this."

"I take it this is your weakness? Your one flaw?" I snicker to myself. How could this man before me have any flaws? He's like Adonis, made into flesh and bone.

"You could say that." He takes a sip through the thick straw. "Are the students still bothering you?" Maverick asks, breaking me out of my thoughts of handsome Greek gods.

"No." I'm quick to answer him, too quick apparently, with the way his eyes flash. Crap.

"Don't lie to me, Emma," he warns, setting his mug down on the tabletop with a clatter. His gaze on me is so intense that I fight the urge to squirm.

"I'm not. They've left me alone. Nobody even talks to me besides Sierra, Ainsley, and Jack. The others treat me like a ghost," I admit bitterly, daring a look over my shoulder to see if the workers or customers are listening. Nobody is. They're too busy staring at the devices in their hands or chatting amongst themselves to have a front-row seat at the drama unfolding before them.

It's one thing to be hated for who my parents are, but it's another thing entirely to be treated as if I don't exist. Passing glances are fleeting and seem to go right through me. I never thought being a loner would bother me this much, but it does. I crave friendships and unity, but what I need above all else is to be one of them. The need for me to fit into the mold this country deems suitable for its citizens blazes through me.

Maverick leans his back against the chair. "It's not a bad thing that they don't talk to you. At least they can't bully you that way."

"You think ignoring someone and pretending they don't exist isn't a form of bullying?" I snap. Crap, I shouldn't have said it like that. Feeling bad, I soften my eyes and lower my voice, "I almost wish they would say something, anything. At least that would make this existence real."

"Real?" Maverick takes another swig of his drink.

"If I were like you, a full immortal, none of this would be happening." My finger traces the small diamond shapes in the glass. Condensation beads up on the outside and drips down to a small puddle forming around it. "Well, maybe some of it, but it wouldn't be as bad."

"No matter what, people can be cruel. It doesn't matter what you look like, who you are, or what you do. Sometimes they need to exploit another being to make them feel worthy of the life they live."

That is a fair point, and I know that. Deep down, I do, but it doesn't change how I feel about it. It doesn't stop the hurtful feelings from emerging.

"Yeah. But it just sucks. This wasn't the warm welcome I had hoped it'd be."

I suck some more of my drink through the straw. Damn, this is good stuff. A new sugary addiction is forming on my end. I haven't found a place here with boba tea, so this may be my temporary go-to drink.

"It'll get better," Maverick replies, glancing around us.

Frowning, I say, "Will it though?"

"Not with that attitude." He reaches across and cups my jaw in his calloused palm. "Just be you. They don't know you yet. You're smart, courageous, and have a heart of gold. If they can't see what an amazing person you are, that's on them."

"Thanks," I murmur.

Heat blooms on my cheeks at his compliment. Maverick's mouth turns to a wicked grin, and I can't help but smile. This man's dimples are my weakness. All he has to do is flash that crooked smile, and I melt like this ice cream in my cup.

"Would you like to go to the range with me?"

"The range?" I question.

He nods. "Where I target practice with my bow. I can teach you to use one."

Swallowing down my unease, I rake in an uneasy breath. "I've never used a weapon before."

I've never needed to back home. There's far more violence and hate in this world than I could've ever imagined. How are humans oblivious to these other beings out there?

"That's okay. I'll show you how."

We haven't gotten that far in my classes yet, but with that hopeful look on his face, who am I to say no?

"Sure?" I answer more like a question.

We arrive at the massive indoor range shortly after grabbing Maverick's bow and several arrows from the house. His excitement is palpable in the air. I watch him notch a blue and silver-tipped arrow, pull it back, and send it flying through the air until it hits the target dead center of the bullseye. Spinning around, he faces me.

"Your turn," he says, handing me the bow in my left hand.

Taking the full weight of the bow, it's lighter than I thought it would be. The weight's about the same as a can of soda. I wrap my palm around the grips and stand at a 90-degree angle like he did.

"Spread these a little more." He nudges my feet apart until they match the width of my shoulders. Placing an arrow into my hand, he continues, "Now, when you're ready, pull the bow up, and place the arrow on the shelf." He points to a small cushioned plastic piece.

I stand up straighter, lift the bow until it's pointed at the target, notch the arrow with my other hand, and lean into the bow. "Now what?"

He stands directly behind me and gently places his hands over mine.

"Use these three fingers to pull back on the string until your hand is perpendicular to your mouth. Keep the tip of your arrow pointed at the center of that bale. Then, when you're ready, release the three fingers holding the string simultaneously."

Sounds easy enough. I inhale deeply through my nose and pull back the string while holding the arrow. Counting to three in my head, I let the air escape from between my lips and release the string. The arrow shoots through the space fast and abruptly stops just outside the largest ring on the target.

"Not bad for your first shot." Maverick grins and hands me another arrow. "Now, try it again. Picture the girls that have been taunting you as the target."

Closing my eyes briefly, I picture Adeline. Long blonde hair and eyes which are the perfect shade of blue. Opening them, I notch the arrow and let it fly. This time, it lands in the red. It's not the inner circle but closer to the center. Several arrows later, I managed to get it about 2 inches from the bull's eye. But my arm is sore from the pressure of pulling the string back.

"Do you want to head back home?" Maverick asks. He must've seen how sluggish the last few arrows were.

"Yeah. I'm exhausted. I was up late studying for tomorrow's exam."

"Which class?"

I sigh. "Biochemistry, AKA the bane of my existence."

He laughs and tosses the bow over his back. Clasping my hand, he replies, "Come on, it can't be that bad?"

"It would be better if the instructor actually knew the material," I huff, falling in step beside him.

"Is it still Professor Edgar?"

I nod. "Is that who you had?"

"Yes, and he was pretty flighty back then. I can't imagine he's gotten much better."

Why does he remain a professor, then? Then it hits me. Professor Edgar has been teaching for over a century. Sierra told me how old Dante is and that he and Maverick met at the academy. Age has never come up between Maverick and me; it hasn't bothered me until now. I gnaw at the inside of my cheek.

"Maverick, can I ask you something?"

"Anything."

Clearing my throat, I ask, "How old are you?"

He stops walking and turns toward me. In the dim lighting, I can barely make out a puzzled look on his face. Is he mad that I asked?

"Are you sure you want to know?" He searches my face.

I nod silently.

"Okay." He sighs. "I'm one hundred and twenty-eight years old."

I can't help it; a gasp sneaks out. "Alright then."

He reaches a warm hand up and tucks a lock of hair behind my ear—the warmth from his fingers like a balm in the cool night breeze.

"I'm still very young for an immortal. Most of us reach a thousand, sometimes two, if we're lucky." His eyebrows bunch together, forming a crease in his forehead as he gauges my reaction.

Letting that soak in, I can't help but think that I'll turn gray and old, and he'll remain unchanged. Would he even want me when I grow old? My throat tightens, and I decide to change the topic.

"What was it like growing up in Graystone?"

As we continue our path home, we discuss how our childhoods differed. Mine in the human world, and his in Graystone. We're about halfway home when the bushes rustle beside us, and I freeze. Maverick straightens his back as he turns toward the woods. A strange squeak comes from really low, and I step back. I don't know what kind of wildlife lives on the island, but I'm not about to be something's lunch.

Maverick tugs me behind him on the sidewalk, putting himself between the woods and me while he simultaneously slides a dagger from his belt. His broad shoulders block my view, but I peer around him, desperate to know what it is. My pulse roars against my eardrums as I fixate on the greenery. Trees and bushes line the long straightaway. It could literally be anything back there. I swallow hard. Do they have bears here?

The branches wiggle again, and a tiny orange kitten pops out of the bottom with another little squeak.

"Oh my god. It's just a cat," I giggle, smacking Maverick's arm lightly, and he laughs.

Squatting down, I hold my hand out for the little guy. His fur is matted, and his tiny little eyes are nearly crusted shut with goopy stuff. The bones of his ribs are poking out far too much.

"Come here, little guy," I coo.

He hesitates briefly before waddling over to me, and I pick him up to get a good look at him. He's nothing but a rack of bones, meaning he's severely malnourished. He's covered in flea bites, and dried blood is piled up in some areas of his skin.

"Are there any more?" I ask Maverick, but he's already looking through the brush.

"I don't see anymore," he answers but continues to search the area for several minutes.

My heart clenches. This poor baby is out here all alone. He likely won't survive for much longer.

"Can I keep him?" His little body is cold, so I cradle him to my chest to try to warm him with my body heat.

Maverick smiles down at me and gently rubs the kitten's head. "Like I said, a heart of gold. Of course, you can keep him. We'll have to go to the store for supplies before bringing him home, though."

The cat snuggles closer to my skin and makes a slight purring noise. I wonder what he was doing out here. Maybe he got separated from his mama. He's too small to be away from her already.

I've never had my own cat before, but I've volunteered at the shelter from time to time. My parents never allowed me to bring any of them home, no matter how much I begged and pleaded with them.

Chapter 5

Ruby

My black lace-up combat boots thud on the concrete path leading to the looming building before me. I used to hate coming here for meetings with the High Council, but today's a new day. I hope. Since Nilo's now the Master Council, I wonder how much has changed. Stepping through the heavy, black steel doors, I'm greeted by a new assistant I've never seen before.

"Your name?" He asks.

"Ruby," I answer.

My gaze sweeps across the creamy white walls with floor-to-ceiling windows, noting everything still looks the same as the last time I was here. I turn back toward the man with a buzzcut and find him looking at me expectantly. I groan internally.

I breathe in deep through my nose before answering, "Ruby Hart."

"Ah, welcome, Ms. Hart. If you'll take a seat right over there, the council's just finishing up." He gestures to the benches that line the hall. "They'll be with you shortly." He gives me a curt nod.

Nobody else is here that I can see. I sit at the farthest leather-clad bench and cross my feet at the ankles. Leaning my head back against the wall, I'm rewarded with silence. No sound comes from the chambers on the other side of the hall. They designed every square inch of this building to be soundproof, even the windows. The meetings I've sat through in that room and the information I've learned over the years is highly classified. Secrets I vowed to take to my grave. I won't break my oath whether I agree with them or not.

Several more immortals start to trickle in through the front door. Each one is told the same thing. I may not recognize their faces, but I know their voice. They're fellow Special Intelligence Agents, ones that, if they choose to stay, I'll be in charge of. No pressure. We exchange pleasantries but say no more. I'm sure they, too, know who I am. My foot bounces on the tile below, and I scrub my sweaty palms on my pants.

The large black doors swing wide, and Nilo emerges wearing traditional black robes that conceal everything besides their hands and faces. He nods to the dozen or so agents who are all sprinkled through the hall, either on the seats or standing.

"We're ready for you." He holds the door open while we all file in, making our way to the first and second rows of chairs directly in front of the dais.

Nilo's steps echo off the vaulted ceilings in the quiet expanse of the room. Us guardians remain standing in a show of respect for our High Council. My hands are clasped together in front of me, just like my fellow agents beside me.

What used to be seven seats that resembled thrones, now only three are raised on a platform behind an ornate red oak divider. In one sits a beautiful female with the hood of her robing off, her long shiny black hair ripples around her in waves. Her dark golden brown skin is accentuated by the gold leaf laurel that rests atop her head.

On the other side of Nilo's empty chair sits a blonde-haired man; he, too, has the hood off. With his creamy pale skin, the green of his eyes looks like emeralds in a desert. Neither of these two were part of the High Council prior to Nilo's command. Nilo really did expunge the crooked officials from our government. I've seen these two in passing, but I can't recall who they are.

Once Nilo reaches his seat, he gestures for all of us to sit. I hate to admit it, but I'm nervous. I know how these things typically go, and the assignments we're given after can sometimes be brutal to complete. Mentally or physically. I've done some shady crap, all in the name of our people. My stomach sours at the thought.

"As you're all aware, Graystone is going through many changes, some of which you can see with your own eyes." He turns to the man beside him. "This is Elias, the liaison to the immortals here in Graystone."

Elias nods. "It's an honor to be here."

Nilo turns to his other side. "And this is Willow, the enchantress to the ancestors."

A witch?

A breath bottles up in my chest as I ponder what's going on. There have only ever been immortals on the High Council. What does this mean going forward? Are witches and warlocks actually going to have a say in our world? And if so, does that mean he's working on having a representative from the other creatures like werewolves, fae, and vampires? My lungs burn, reminding me to breathe and not get too carried away.

She smiles and nods to all of us as if my head isn't about to implode with the possibilities of what a new Graystone looks like.

"As of right now, we are the only High Council of Graystone. In an effort to save our beloved country, I've brought you all here because you've shown impeccable skills and loyalty to the citizens who live in this country. You hold our values above your own, sometimes at the cost of your life. I don't believe in blind teamwork." He shakes his head. "You need to know who has your back. We must stand united for the citizens to see us for who we are."

Murmurs break out from the others around me, and my breaths continue to rattle in and out. I never thought I'd see a time when my friendship with Alex wouldn't be condemned.

Nilo continues, "In the name of transparency, look around you. These are your fellow Special Intelligence Agents that you formerly only knew by a number."

I cast a fleeting glance at the others. I was given the perfect opportunity to study them as each one arrived.

"I want to introduce you to the new SIA Captain, Ruby, formerly known as Agent Nine."

Raising my hand up, I wave to them all, feeling like I'm back in elementary school. I can feel their watchful gazes on me like a heat trailing over my skin. I knew Nilo was going to announce the new role today, but I didn't expect the anxiousness that floods through me at this moment.

"She will be your point of contact and the one who will provide your assignments." He scans each of them. "If any of you object to this change of leadership, you can leave now and forfeit your title of SIA."

Not even a shuffle of shoes on the tile floor reach my ears. To my surprise, not one guardian makes any movement to leave or voices their opposition. Letting out the breath I held slowly, the reality starts sneaking in. This is it. I'm finally going to be able to change the home I love into something more. A rush of giddiness flows through my veins, wiping away the anxiety and making me feel light and happy.

In a world that can assault you with tragedies and hardships, each and every thing that brings you joy is equally monumental.

"Take the weekend to prepare for your new roles. We'll reconvene first thing Monday morning at the Guard. And one more thing: your titles are no longer confidential. The citizens of Graystone deserve our transparency."

After the dismissal, there's only one place I can think of to celebrate. The blue benitoite stone is cool against my palm as I follow the others into the bright, sunlit courtyard. Birds are chirping a melody in the distance as a slight breeze blows around me. The intoxicating scent of blooming lilacs and peonies that encircle the grounds is a delicacy like no other.

Graystone is truly magical at any time of year. The flowers and other plant life bloom and thrive at all times. Some of that is due to our witches, who have an affinity for horticulture. After all, many spells and potions utilize the plants that grow abundantly here.

"I'll see you guys on Monday." I wave to the others before the portal in front of me swirls around and around. Once the stone building is in view, I step through and try to contain the fluttering sensation in my stomach.

The bell rings above the door but is quickly drowned out by voices, clattering pans, and orders being called through the small window that separates the seating area from the kitchen. My gaze lands on him as if compelled to do so. Eric's back is to me, but I know it's him from the ebony hair to the muscled torso covered only by a black t-shirt and down to his dark wash jeans. He's like a beacon compared to the others inside.

I watch silently as he takes a pair of women's orders. His pen moves quickly across the small notebook in his hand. The smile that the blonde flashes and the fake high-pitched laugh grate on my nerves. Even if I didn't recognize Eric from the back, the way other women look at him would give him away. I have a feeling it's like that everywhere for him.

Even though many immortals distrust Eric or his last name, I should say. It hasn't stopped the ladies from wanting to bed him. I shouldn't be angry with them; that morally gray thing he's got going on also works for me. Against my better judgment, I might add. It doesn't help that he's cocky yet charming at the same time. A man who is that confident is a dangerous thing. I sigh and nibble on my bottom lip.

Eric tucks the notebook and pen into his back pocket and grabs some empty dishes from the table beside them. He turns, and his sapphire eyes instantly lock on mine. My stomach does a freefall as a slow smile forms on his lips. The memory of that heated kiss we shared is seared into the forefront of my brain. My mouth goes dry at the thought. Everybody else blurs away as if I have tunnel vision. There's a heat in his eyes I've never seen before in any other man, making me question everything.

A male's loud voice calls out, snapping us out of the trance we're in. Eric holds a finger up to tell me to wait as he brings the tub through the swinging doors to the back room. I'm left standing here with my heart beating at a thunderous pace. Suddenly, it's so hot in here. I tug my sleeves up in an effort to cool down.

Eric

It's the typical Friday night dinner rush, and we're short-staffed. I'm bussing tables and being one of only two waiters on duty. Now that all the guests are seated and their orders are placed, a lull will be ahead. Which I can not wait for. That's my time to take my break, sit out back of the building, and just be alone. The crowd gets to me more now than it ever has.

These blubbering broads in front of me are no different. I'm usually a shameless flirt, but not here in a country I barely know or around people who don't want me here. I know I'm no saint; my past confirms that. I just want a fresh start. Besides the bullying she's faced, Emma loves it here. I don't want to be far from my sister, even if she's staying at Maverick's place for the time being.

The blonde woman to my right leans forward, no doubt trying to get me to look down at her low-cut shirt. The old me? I probably would've. It's not her fault she doesn't have scarlet hair and deep brown eyes. It doesn't help that the blonde resembles the girl giving Emma a hard time. Instead, I swing my gaze to the one seated across from her. At least she's not as obvious in her advances.

"Is there anything else I can get for you ladies?"

"Oh, there's something alright," the blonde says before she cackles like a damn witch.

A muscle tics in my jaw. The high-pitched sound is like metal scraping the pavement. Highly irritating and disturbing at the same time. Turning my head back to the skanky one, I narrow my eyes and fight the urge to be an asshole.

"From the menu," I clarify.

When no answer comes, I reply dryly, "Your food will be out soon."

Twisting away from the women, the table beside them is still full of dirty dishes. Jonah's on his break, so I'm handling everything for the time being.

Placing the last dirty dishes in the tub, I turn toward the front to check for diners waiting to be seated when I see her. Ruby nervously chews at her bottom lip while I seem to have forgotten how to talk, breathe, and be anything but right here. This woman puts a spell on me every time I see her.

She's wearing tight-fitting black tactical pants with a matching long-sleeve. Her weapons still hang from a belt wrapped around her slim waist. Damn, she looks like a hot assassin. I now have new content for the fantasies in my head. Ruby's staring back at me with an unreadable expression on her face. A tingling sensation erupts across my skin.

Momentarily, I forget what I'm doing until Nelson barks out, "Table five's ready."

Holding up a finger to Ruby, I rush back to dump the tub for Felix to wash and grab the serving tray full of plates and drinks. I've gotten good at balancing the weight of these. Quickly delivering the tray back to the cook station, I head to the hostess stand in the front where Ruby waits.

"Hey, Ruby. Are you dining in tonight or to go?" Please say dining in, I add silently.

She looks around the packed diner and asks, "Are there even any tables free?"

"There's one over there, I just have to wipe it down."

"Okay. Dining in then." She grins, and I fight the urge to fist-pump the sky.

I snag a clean washcloth and rush back to the table, where I just grabbed the empty plates. Cleaning that table with a speed that would make my boss's head spin, I gesture for Ruby to come sit. The menus are underneath a thin glass sheet covering the oak tables. Most of the diners know the offerings by heart and don't even need to look at them. Apparently, the owner isn't big on switching things up. But hey, whatever works. This place is always busy, but the food is great.

"Do you know what you want, or do you need a few minutes?"

"I know what I want," she starts, "I'll take a-"

"Can I get a refill?" the one who can't keep her tits put away cuts off Ruby in a sickening voice.

Ruby rolls her eyes as she taps her crimson-colored nails on the tabletop.

"Ignore her; she'll wait her turn," I coax Ruby to keep going.

"I'll take the spaghetti with a side of garlic bread and a glass of red wine, please."

"Excuse me? Waiter?" the blonde calls out louder as if she didn't hear me a second ago.

"I'll be right there," I reply, gritting my teeth. I jot Ruby's order down on the slip for the cooks, and tell her, "Once Jonah's back from his break, I'll come sit with you. I'm sorry, but unfortunately, it's hectic right now."

"I asked for a refill," the blonde one says in a snippy tone.

"No need to apologize, you're working. I get it." Ruby flashes a sympathetic smile.

I wink at her before turning away and stopping at the annoying woman's table.

"I heard you the first time when you rudely interrupted my other customer. Now, will that be a refill for both or just yours?" I peg her with a hard stare.

"Mine and you can't call your customers rude."

This woman's attitude went from obnoxiously flirty to snotty once Ruby walked through that door. I don't tolerate anybody giving me an attitude for no reason. I especially won't allow them to treat Ruby that way.

"Why not?" I ask with a straight face.

"Your job as a waiter is to ensure the diners are satisfied with their meal, not ignoring them."

"Ah, so you did hear me. And yet you continued to interrupt her." I tsk while shaking my head.

"Maybe Lonnie should know how unsatisfied our service has been," she snaps. "Where is he?"

"Karen? Can I assume that's your name? You know, with the short blonde hair and entitled bitch attitude, it seems fitting."

Ruby chokes on a laugh, then coughs trying to cover it up. Everybody goes silent in the restaurant. Even the employees in the back room cease to make any noise.

She gasps. "I'm going to have your job for this!"

The brunette she came with shrinks back and tries to hide her reddening face behind her hand. This must not be the first time something like this has happened.

"Honestly, I don't give a fuck. I don't deserve to be snapped at, and the other diners deserve to order their meals in peace and not feel rushed."

"Wow. It's true what they say about you, you really are an ass, following right in your father's footsteps."

My eyebrows raise of their own accord. She didn't just go there. Count to three; let it go. I'm trying to be a better man. I can do better. Ruby's right here witnessing everything. Be the better person. I twist the rag in my hand until I feel the threads fraying and snapping.

You know what? Fuck it.

"Did daddy not love you, not give you enough attention? Is it because I'm such an ass that just ten minutes ago you were trying to push your nasty tits out for me to see?" Her face turns crimson, and her mouth falls open in a gasp. "Even though I clearly wasn't interested, you were coming on to me so hard I'm sure the whole diner saw it."

"Do you even know who I am?" she shouts, standing up to try to get in my face when she's all of five foot two and barely reaches my chin.

"No," I scoff. "And I don't care to. You should take a page from her book," I point at Ruby, who I notice looks like she's going to swing at her any minute. "She doesn't have to show an inch of skin for me to want her. And she sure as hell treats everyone with respect."

"Why would I want to be like her? She's a fucking weirdo." Her face crinkles in disgust.

My blood begins to boil under my skin. Ruby steps out of her seat, but I hold a forearm out to block her from getting involved.

"Let me go, Eric," Ruby demands in a low menacing tone.

"As much as I'd love to watch her rock your world, your meals have been canceled. Get the fuck out."

"You don't have the authority to do that," she snarls.

"No. But I do. Kindly remove yourself from my property," my boss's thunderous voice fills the room.

Shit! He must've heard the whole thing. Yup, I'm losing my job for sure.

"I'm reporting all of you!" she screams as her friend tugs her out the door.

"We'll survive," he replies dryly, gesturing to the rest of the diners, who begin to laugh.

Once the door swings closed, the entire restaurant erupts in clapping and cheers. It seems nobody else liked her either.

I slowly turn to my boss, "Sir, I was out of line-"

"You weren't. I saw the whole thing. My staff are like family to me, and nobody gets away with treating them like that." He glances at Ruby. "My customers as well. We don't need people like that here. You're the only one who had the balls to stand up to her."

"Table ten?" Nelson calls. No doubt they heard it all in there too.

"Wrap it up. We'll donate it," Lonnie answers Nelson before turning back to me. "And Eric?"

"Yeah, boss man?"

"Dinner's on the house."

I order my meal, and once it's ready, I carry mine and Ruby's to our table. The guests are right back to chattering loudly, and Jonah's back from his dinner break.

Ruby tells me all about what happened at the council building earlier, and I'm impressed. I knew Ruby was amazing, but leading a special team? Damn, she's so far out of my league it's disheartening.

"What do you think Graystone will turn into?" I ask. It's not like I know much about what it's like now. I usually keep to myself.

"I hope it'll turn into a safe place for all beings, not just for immortals and witches. I want it to feel like home for everyone but still be safe." Ruby casts a glance around the restaurant and all the people inside. "Most of all, I want to give the children of Graystone a land they can thrive in and a government that'll protect them."

I nod in understanding before biting a chunk of fried chicken. Turning her words over in my mind while I chew, it's as if a puzzle piece clicks into place. *A government that'll protect them.* What happened to Ruby stems from her childhood, and Graystone's leaders didn't protect her as they should.

She's picking at her food as I watch her turn from this beautiful woman into a tiny spitfire of a child right before my eyes. The wind is knocked from my lungs as possibilities of what could've happened to her slam into me like a shotgun. Image after image, shot after shot, I'm nearly gutted with the what-ifs.

Ruby looks up from her plate and meets my watchful gaze, and she's right back to the woman I adore when she smirks before saying, "You wanna picture ghost boy?"

"I'm proud of you," I tell her the words I desperately wanted to hear as a child. "For everything you've done and what you have yet to accomplish."

"Thanks." A blush stains her cheeks.

The urge to take her painful childhood memories away, even just a smidge flares to life. "How can I help make Graystone a better place?"

"You want to help?"

Her answering smile means everything to me. There's not much I wouldn't do to make Ruby happy.

"I want to make this place everything you want it to be. Maybe the place we both should've grown up in?" I hedge.

Her brown eyes widen and I know, without a doubt, this country failed her at her weakest point. She takes a sip of her red wine and avoids looking at me.

Wiping my mouth with my napkin, I lean back in the booth. "What's going on in that pretty head of yours?" I ask quietly.

"I'm more than just a guardian, and you see that you see me." She shrugs as if it's not often somebody acknowledges the person underneath that devil-may-care attitude.

"And you don't try to make me be anything besides myself," I reply truthfully. Ruby hasn't once pushed me to change my ways. She accepts me for who I am.

"Can I ask you something?" She twirls her fork around the spaghetti on her plate.

"Anything."

"Hypothetically speaking, if we were to be together." Ruby pauses and swallows. "If Sierra told you she wanted you, what would you do?"

Yup. I was not expecting that to be the question. I can't say I blame her, though. Is she really thinking of being with me as more than just friends? Hope surges through me at the thought. I debate my answer before I open my mouth to speak. If I only have one shot at this, it better be my best. And I'm ready to fire.

"I won't lie to you, I loved Sierra. But it's more of an echo now, like an ache. She was never meant to be mine, and I've accepted that." I pause and lean my arms on the table, gazing at the woman across from me and feeling a wave of emotions bubbling up. "The more time I spend with you makes it seem as if it were all supposed to happen this way. That all of the misplaced love I had for her is what brought me to you."

CHAPTER 6

Sierra

My eyes snap open to the sound of a child giggling close by. Huh, I'm back at Dante's cabin, I realize as I stretch my arms above my head. Last I knew, I went to sleep in my dorm room back at the academy, weird. I've been exhausted lately. I can't even remember what happened last night. Unfortunately, that's been happening far too often. I sit up in bed, rubbing the sleep out of my eyes, and throw my robe over my silk nightgown. Padding over to the door, I quietly open it a few inches, and the laughing gets louder.

The laugh sounds familiar. Tilting my head toward the narrow hall, my forehead wrinkles as I try to think of who could be in our house. I don't know any kids. Unless it's one of Dante's friends, I haven't met yet. I hold my breath, standing as still as possible, waiting for the child to talk or giggle again so I can figure it out.

"Again! Again!" The little one says. God, he sounds so familiar. Where the heck do I know him from? I dig through all the memories in my head, desperately trying to remember.

I start creeping down the hall on my tiptoes, trying my damnedest to be quiet while I eavesdrop. The next laugh I hear stops me in my tracks with a sharp intake of air.

No. It can't be. She's dead. I watched her die. I saw them carry her casket through the honor guard and into the church.

My feet move of their own accord, and I dart to the end of the hallway and freeze as if a bucket of ice water is dropped over my head. My feet are planted below me and rooting me to the spot, as my eyes are stuck on one person.

"*Mom?*" I whimper.

My mom's standing in front of the stove with a frying pan in her hand, tossing pancakes into the air just like she used to do back home.

"Mama, Gigi's here!" The boy's voice snaps me out of the vortex, spinning around the image of my mother wailing in agony at Excalibur's hand as a fireball torched her from inside.

My gaze finally lands on the little boy. Almost black hair, with hazel eyes that are exactly like my own. Mine and Dante's son from the vision Teiresias showed me when we reinforced the spell that keeps Excalibur imprisoned. He's slightly younger, but he's definitely my son. My blood runs cold, and my palms begin to sweat.

What the hell?

This isn't real. It has to be a dream. Am I in one of Teiresias's visions? But it's all wrong; they can't see me in those. All I can do is watch them. They've never interacted with me. My chest heaves in breaths as if starving for oxygen. I feel like I'm drowning.

"Are you okay, Sierra?" my mother says as she places the frying pan down and heads toward me, a frown on her face.

Before I know it, she wraps her arms around me, and I instinctively do the same to her. She's so warm, and the faint trace of her floral perfume invades my nose. It all feels so real. I've never felt anything this concrete in a dream, even the ones that Dante creates. There's always been a dulling of the senses while in a dream. I squeeze her harder. Her breath breezes across my neck as she pulls away.

"Are you really here?" I ask as my voice cracks on the last word.

"Yes, sweetheart. I'm here. I thought you could use the extra help since Dante's away on an assignment." Her lips tilt up slowly as her eyes dance across my face.

"But, I saw... I watched you die." I almost choke on the words. A large lump lodges in my throat, making it hard to get a breath through. My vision blurs as I take in every tiny detail of her.

"I assure you I am very much alive. Would I be able to make my grandson his favorite blueberry pancakes if I wasn't?" Her delicate brown eyebrows pinch together, and her smile disappears. Her eyes search every inch of my face.

At this, the boy claps and says, "More Gigi, more cakes."

I exhale slowly, walking over to him in his high chair printed with safari animals on it. He opens his arms wide, wanting me to hug him. I lean down, and he wraps his tiny little arms around me. I don't even care that they're sticky with maple syrup. I rub his back and place a kiss on his forehead, inhaling the soft scent of baby shampoo.

Wanting to busy myself with something, I get up and make my way to the coffee maker on the counter and pour myself a hefty amount. Maybe caffeine will help this fog that's settled over me. I wish Dante were here. He'd make everything okay. My anima gemella would help me understand what the heck is going on.

"Where did you say Dante was again?" I ask.

"He's on a mission overseas. Are you alright, Sierra?" Mom reaches a hand out to my forearm and gently grasps it. Her fingers are warm where they touch my skin.

"I just don't," I start, not knowing how to say it. Looking over at Dante's mini-me, I think he must be around two years old. "I just don't remember anything. It's like the past few years are just... gone." I shake my head, trying to clear whatever has me so jumbled, but it's useless. It only proves to make the pounding ache behind my temples thump harder.

"Oh, sweetheart, that's normal with a TBI," she says, placing her other hand on my shoulder. Her facial features morph into the concerned mother look she'd get whenever I was hurt growing up.

"A TBI?" What's normal? Losing two years or more of memories?

"Yes, you suffered a traumatic brain injury about a month or so ago when the humans bombed the training facility you were teaching at."

"A bomb?" I squeak.

She nods solemnly. I press the heel of my palm into my eyes. How do I not know that? What the hell is going on around here?

"The blast threw you into the cement wall, and you were in a coma for two weeks." She takes a deep breath and glances at the toddler. Her face tightens, and wrinkles form around her eyes. Then she continues quieter, "We didn't know if you were going to pull through."

My mind races a million miles an hour trying to process everything she's saying. I have a kid. I'm a teacher. The school was bombed.

"Why did the humans bomb us?"

"Maybe we should talk about that later. Here, eat up. You need your strength." She places a plate on the table for me.

Three large blueberry pancakes beckon me, but I have no appetite. I usually love food. They smell good and look delicious, but I can't bring myself to grab a forkful and put it in my mouth.

I sit beside him at the table and watch my mom pour more pancake batter into the hot pan. I sit there silently, taking it all in. Could my memory of the past be wrong? Did she live through that battle? I don't remember even having a child. I rub my cheeks, trying to will myself to remember. The only memory that surfaces is just her dying and the funeral. That was the last I saw of her besides in the scenes Teiresias showed me.

And my son?

I don't even know his name, and I'm too ashamed of that fact to ask what it is. What kind of mother doesn't remember her own child? A deep sigh exits my throat before I lean back in the chair and rest my eyes. The headache pounds in sync with my beating heart. At least one thing's consistent, I guess. My breaths slow, and warmness surrounds me like a cocoon. I yawn and relax deeper into the chair.

When my eyes open again, I'm in my bed at the academy, gasping for breath.

What the hell was that? I glance at Emma's twin bed across the room and find she's sound asleep. My mom was there? And my son? Is Teiresias showing me the afterlife? That wouldn't make sense, tho, if my son is there. He hasn't been born, so how could he have died? Or is it more of a holding place for all of them?

Settling my breathing, I gingerly get out of bed, noting my body is still pretty sore from the beating I put it through yesterday. Even though immortals heal fast, we can still suffer from delayed onset muscle soreness, or DOMS, as my instructor calls it. I slowly slide my bureau drawer open, trying not to let it squeak on the rollers. I grab out a set of joggers and a tank top. Snaking my earbuds out of the nightstand, I tiptoe out of the room and pad down the stairs to the main doors of the academy.

The cool autumn air surrounds me. Shoving the buds into my ears, I put on my favorite rock playlist and stretch out my achy muscles on the side of the track. I was never a fan of running before my training in the Caribbean. Now, it's a way to process my thoughts and beat my frustrations into the dirt.

After I've made three laps around the track, my heart rate begins to speed up. My sneakers pound into the ground to the beat blasting in my ears. My mind turns fuzzy as I try to recall what brought me here. I know a dream awoke me, but what was it?

It has something to do with my mom; I know that much by the amount of grief that sits below my skin. I search deeper into my memory, digging through layers and layers of memories, but nothing comes to me. Huh. I hate it when that happens. It's not the first time, and I'm sure it won't be the last, but I can't get rid of the feeling that this one was really important.

I needed to remember that dream.

Emma

My heeled shoes tap on the tile as I walk down the corridor. The halls that are usually filled with students are eerily silent. The entire school is in quiet mode for testing. Stifling a yawn, I fight the urge to go back to my dorm and take a nap.

I've had a hard time sleeping lately. It's never felt more real to me that life is short. My life, that is, until now. I'll age, Maverick won't. Neither will Sierra or Eric.

There's so much I feel I need to make up for because my father was a shitty person. I wonder if I'll have enough time to be able to atone for his sins. I know other half-breeds have gone through the transition to become immortal. I've toyed with the idea but never gave it any real credit.

But now I'm seriously debating the possibility of becoming a full immortal.

Even though today is typically a school day, I only had half my classes. I finished my semester exams this morning, making my afternoon free. Pushing through the frosted glass doors to the academy's library, the familiar scent of worn pages with a hint of vanilla greets me. Nobody else is in here, at least from what I can tell. Several small tables encircle the room for students to do their work. The ones closest to me are empty.

I scan the signage above the bookcases for something that'll point me in the right direction. I've only visited this library for specific books needed for my classes. Usually, I avoid anything to do with the Guardian Academy in my free time. I don't trust any of the students or staff here. None of the girls that bullied me even got a detention. Only Sierra was punished. Thrusting those thoughts out of my mind, instead, I focus on what I'm here to do.

"Would it be considered medical or history?" I mumble to myself.

"Can I help you, dear?" The sweet, older librarian asks. Her hair is speckled with a few grays, and the neutral shades of her pencil skirt and blouse blend into the bookcases and walls behind her.

"Ummm." Holy buckets, what do I say? The lights are suddenly too bright in here. "I'm studying ancient rituals for a project," the lie slips out easily.

She pushes the glasses farther up her nose. "What kind of rituals?"

The feeling of ants crawling across my skin erupts everywhere. I've never been a good liar and am unsure how to find what I need without help. My cheeks begin to heat with a flush.

"The transition into an immortal."

"Hmph. I wasn't aware any classes held that assignment." She studies me like a lab rat, her eyes narrowing behind the thick glasses.

She knows I'm lying; I can feel it—saliva pools in my mouth. I think I'm going to be sick. My palms begin to sweat and itch.

Shaking my head, I continue to lie, "It's for extra credit, ma'am. Not one on the curriculum."

Will she check into this? I cross my toes in my sneakers. Please don't ask me what class it is. I don't want to say any more than I have to.

"You'll find we don't have much on that subject. But, what we have can be found in the history section."

"Thank you so much!"

I twist on my feet and nearly dart down that aisle. I don't need her prying even more out of me. The history section is massive; it spans about ten feet long and six feet high. I scan the spines from top to bottom, left to right, and find one that lists "Rituals of the ancestors" as the title. That sounds promising. Pulling it free, I notice the hardback is worn on the edges, and the corners are no longer sharp. It's had a lot of use.

Placing my bag on an empty table, I sit and rummage through to find my notebook. As I stare at the leather cover of the old book, my cell phone buzzes in my pocket.

"Where are you?" Ainsley's text reads.

"Library," I type out.

It buzzes again. "Want company?"

I debate on telling her no, but I'd feel bad turning her down. And she may understand; after all, she's a half-breed as well.

"Sure," I reply and set my phone on the table face down.

Flipping over the cover and the first few pages, I find an index. As I skim over the words, nothing jumps out at me. So, instead, I start to read over the first few pages quickly. Most of it so far has just been items they use during rituals. I thumb through several more before I find protection rituals.

"Whatcha doing?" Ainsley asks, dropping her backpack on the floor beside me.

I jump hard enough to hit my elbow on the table. Ainsley giggles, causing me to scowl at her. The librarian pokes her head around a bookcase and shushes us. I don't know why; we're the only ones here right now. Who could we possibly be too loud for? God forbid a student laughs in here. Fun sucker.

Ainsley pulls the chair out beside me, sits, and looks at the text before me. Then, her eyes scan over the words written in the notebook. Transition is scrawled across the top with two columns below, pros and cons. I nonchalantly turn the page.

"Are you doing what I think you are?" she questions, leaning her arms on the table.

Caught red-handed, I nod. How else would I explain what I'd written down?

She relaxes her shoulders. "Oh good! I thought I was the only one trying to figure it out."

"Figure what out?" I ask just in case.

She looks at me as if I have a horn coming out of my forehead. "How we can transition without dying," she whispers, smacking a hand against her forehead.

Phew! That took a load off me.

"You want to also?" I say, keeping my voice barely above a whisper.

"Of course! Why wouldn't I?"

"The chances are slim for us," I remind us of the grim reality we'd face if we went through with it.

"I know. But others have done it successfully." Hope fills her eyes, and a smile graces her mouth.

There's a creak in the floorboards behind us. When I turn around, I don't see anybody there. Immortals have enhanced hearing, and I'd rather keep this research on the down low. I don't know if the librarian is an immortal, half-breed, or something else entirely.

On a fresh sheet of paper, I write, "Let's not talk here. Just write it down."

Ainsley nods in understanding, and we skim over the pages together in silence. A few people come in, grab some books to check out for the long weekend, and leave. Nobody bothers us, but I can't help but feel like we're being watched. The hairs on the back of my neck randomly stand up, and goosebumps cover my arms.

After a couple of hours of staring at the texts, the words blur together. We both wrote down some notes, but most of the information in the books wasn't helpful.

"I think the Repository would have other resources. It's huge enough that we could probably get lost in it. Do you want to meet there on Sunday and see what we can find out?" Ainsley asks as I tuck my notebook into my bag.

Probably not a bad idea. While this library is vast, it lacks the research we're looking for, just as the librarian said.

"Sure," I agree before we part ways.

Ainsley stays on campus all year. She hasn't mentioned her mom, and what she's said about her dad doesn't paint a good picture of him. If she'd rather stay at the academy than at home, that tells me how bad her home life was. I know my dad won't ever win Father of the Year, but at least he loved me and never made me feel unwelcome in my own house.

Once I'm back to Maverick's house, I find it empty except for the little fur ball lying in his bed next to the door. I'm not surprised; Maverick always seems to be working. I know his job is important, but it still sucks. The kitten stretches out and begins purring as I rub his chin. At least somebody's happy to see me.

"How's my handsome little man?"

He nudges my hand as I start to pull it away. I scoop him up and carry him to the kitchen while he bats playfully at my hair.

"Are you hungry, Sparky?"

We named him that because once he had some food in him, he ran all over the house with a spunkiness cats with his health don't typically have. As soon as I set him down and pop the top off a can of soft food, he weaves in and out of my legs, meowing like crazy.

"I know, buddy, it's coming."

I'll keep what Ainsley and I are researching to myself for a while. I hate hiding things from Maverick and Sierra, but I'd rather have more concrete information before I bring it up to them. On my way home, I poked my head into Graystone's Repository, and Ainsley wasn't exaggerating its size. I can't wait until Sunday to dive into the epic amount of books they hold.

Chapter 7

Dante

I'm worried about Sierra. She's been pushing herself so hard at the academy and all her extra training lessons that she's always exhausted. All she ever wants to do is sleep. I rub the back of my neck as a cold chill sweeps through my body. I feel like there's more to it than just being tired.

I've tried dreamwalking with her several times while she's been sleeping, and it's as if she's not even in the dream realm. Even with our anima gemella bond, I can't locate her in that vast openness. I've never had that happen to me before. It's like I'm being blocked. Something's not right. I just can't put my finger on it.

Ring. Ring. The shrill tone of my cell phone draws my attention to the screen. It's Reid returning my call.

"Hey Reid, how are you?"

"I'm well, my friend, and you?" he answers in his smooth tone.

"I could be better; I've got a lot on my mind lately," I reply honestly.

Isn't that the understatement of the year? This whole past year has been like a never-ending roller coaster ride.

"I gathered that from your message." He pauses. "You think something's wrong with Sierra?"

"Yeah." I nod even though he can't see it. "I just can't shake this feeling that something's off."

"How so?"

I pace between the living room and kitchen of our log cabin. I've felt restless all day and can't sit still for the life of me. Today's my day off, and Sierra was stuck in classes all day. Having nothing to focus my mind on isn't a good thing at the moment.

"Well, I know she's been studying and having extra training sessions at the academy, but that shouldn't make her as drained as she is. Even on the weekends, when she comes home, she goes to bed early and wakes up late."

"It could be depression. Have you tried talking to her about it?"

"I have, and all she ever says is that she's tired but fine. The most concerning part is that I'm unable to dreamwalk with her. It's as if she's not in the dream realm but elsewhere." I scratch at my chin.

That's the most puzzling part. It's similar to when her parents were being dosed with iron while held captive. Sierra can still use her magic, so I know it's not that.

"I don't know much about the dream realm, unfortunately, but maybe her body is just trying to heal itself, and being in such a deep sleep means there are no disturbances. Could it be she's learning how to shield her mind?"

I turn Reid's words over in my mind several times. That could be it. I forgot I wasn't able to dreamwalk with her when she was going through the transition, either.

"I don't know, maybe." My gut's telling me there's more to it, and its never steered me wrong before.

If Sierra is learning how to protect her mind from intruders, it would be something we could all use. The amount of guardians, werewolves, and vampires Excalibur was able to mind control before is terrifying. My ribs tighten against my lungs, and my stomach roils as a new thought occurs to me.

He was able to absorb the magic from others; who's to say another being didn't siphon his as well?

"Tell you what," Reid's voice snaps me back to reality. "I'm in England participating in some panels. I'll talk amongst my colleagues here and see if they have any knowledge of the dream realm."

"Thanks, Reid."

"Anytime."

Sierra should be here anytime now. Her last class ended an hour ago, but she's been staying after to work with Audrey and Zuri. Maybe some manual labor will help. Throwing my boots on, I head out to the stack of firewood that's blocked on the side of the house. Once I have a chunk of wood upright, I grab the splitting mall and swing it high over my head. The log busts into two pieces. Straightening it again, I split each one into smaller chunks to use in the fireplace.

Here in Graystone, over the winter time, it can get down to forty or so degrees at night. The daytime still climbs back up into the seventies or eighties, but the fireplace will help take the edge off the chilly nights. After I split everything I had previously blocked up with my chainsaw, I head back to the house to get a drink.

Thoughts of another being with Excalibur's power on the loose take over my every thought. We can never go back to a world that didn't have the constant threat of him returning.

Footsteps sound on my front porch moments before it opens. Sierra walks through, stifling a yawn.

"Hey, beautiful."

"Hey, handsome."

Walking up before her, I take the backpack slung over her shoulder and place it on the hook by the door. Wrapping my arms around her, I tug her in close and take several large, deep breaths of her scent. She smells like home to me.

I nuzzle her neck and confess, "I've missed you this week."

"Me too," she admits as she snuggles in closer. "You smell good."

I chuckle. "Glad to know you like the smell of sweat and wood."

Sierra pulls back and crinkles her nose. "You are a little sweaty." She sucks in her bottom lip to try to hide the grin forming.

"Well, I was bored waiting around for you." I grin back at her.

"I'm sorry. Yuri kept me for longer than I thought she would." Sierra snatches an apple off the counter and sinks her teeth into it.

"Is everything okay?"

"Yeah, she was just teaching me how to divert flood waters, which sounds easier than it is. I don't think the creek behind the Guardian Academy will ever be the same." She laughs, and there's a twinkle in her eyes I love seeing.

I shake my head and smirk. "Oh no. What did you do?"

Sierra covers her mouth with a hand and snickers. "I may have made some spots deep enough you could lose a car in."

"May have?" I prompt, gazing down at her with my eyebrows drawn up.

"I plead the fifth." A wicked grin stretches across her face before biting into the apple again.

"We don't have those amendments here." I shake my head and lean forward, snatching a mouthful of the crisp snack in her hand.

"Well, if that's the case, the school is also the proud owner of a tiny waterfall." She giggles.

Hating to break the moment but desperate to know, I ask, "Has Yuri been teaching you how to shield your mind?"

An inward, thoughtful expression crosses her face before she answers, "No. Why?"

A sinking feeling settles into my stomach. I was hoping the answer was that easy.

"I've tried dreamwalking with you several times and can never find you there."

"Huh. That's weird. I haven't been sleeping very well; maybe that's why?"

Not wanting to frighten her, I tell her, "Maybe."

While I wait for Reid, I'll continue to dig into everything I can on my end. There has to be something blocking it.

Sierra

Thwack! Another one of Audrey's punishing blows lands on my thigh. Pain radiates down to my toes as I twist to dodge her next hit. This position puts the bright sunshine directly in my line of sight. Faking a left, I dart to my right, and the sun is once again on my side. Sweat beads up on my face and trickles down in a salty trail.

"Hey Audrey, can I ask you something?" I say around my heavy breathing.

We've been sparring for nearly an hour. I'm covered in sweat and panting like a dog, but she's hardly breaking a sweat. It's not even close to being a fair fight.

"Of course," she answers, swinging a right hook and barely catching the headgear at my chin.

Straightening my headgear, I contemplate how to word what I'm asking. It seems so far-fetched; she may label me as a lunatic. Who knows, I may be.

"Have you ever had dreams that felt so real," I begin before heaving in another breath, "When you wake up, you don't know which is real?"

Audrey's face tightens behind the head protection, but I can still see her lips forming a thin line. "I've had some that've felt pretty realistic. Are they like flashbacks?"

Landing a blow to her side, she winces and rushes to block my next advance. My rubber stake slams into her chest where her heart is and bends easily. We've only recently begun to use these in her class. These rubber replicas of the real thing are training us to use the real stakes for an upcoming class. Other students have told me how realistic the vampire dummies look. Seeing them in real life is a whole different ball game, though. I don't think anything can prepare you for that.

"No. Like a totally different life," I pant out the answer.

She looks at me, puzzled, and stops bouncing on her feet. "I've had some strange dreams in the past. Do they feel like nightmares?"

How in the world can she still carry on a conversation without getting winded?

"I don't know." I pause, trying to think of how to explain them. "It's almost as if I'm living two different lives."

Her eyes search my face far longer than necessary. Pinpricks break out along my skin. Maybe I shouldn't have said anything.

Wrinkles form around her eyes, and her tone softens as she asks, "Is the other one a bad life?"

"Not really," I say truthfully, shaking my head.

If they were, I wouldn't be having this problem. It would be too easy to cast those dreams as just nightmares. Images of my mother and son float through my vision, and I close my eyes tightly in an effort to keep them there. I don't remember what happens in the dreams, but I know they're there. Once the images disappear, I open my eyes to find Audrey watching me. Her eyes seem distant, cast off in some other memory of her own.

She drops her arms to her sides. Apparently, she's done kicking my ass for the day. "Do you think this one is bad?"

My eyes meet hers, and I hesitate before replying, "I wouldn't say bad, but there's room for improvement."

Her gaze flicks to the other students walking across the grounds. School's been out for nearly two hours, but it's a weekday, so we're all stuck here. We're only permitted to leave with Headmaster Matias's approval, and he doesn't seem to approve many.

"How about you write them all in a journal, like diary entries? Dreams can mean a lot of different things. Some people believe that when you dream, your subconscious is trying to tell you something. Maybe you can piece it all together by getting it all on paper."

"Huh. I never thought of that. As the day progresses, I often forget most of it."

"So, write it down as soon as you wake up while all the details are fresh in your mind. The campus store has a bunch of notebooks and journals you'd probably like." She smiles warmly, tugs her headgear off, and reaches for mine.

Parting ways, I stalk toward the main building. I've only been in the academy's store half a dozen times. They don't have a lot; it's mainly T-shirts and other clothing with the school's name on them. I search the aisles until I find the stationery section.

My fingertips brush along the covers of the notebooks, all lined up evenly. The words, find your destiny, pop out at me. The background image is a galaxy of beautiful shades of purple and blue. Some stars are scattered in there as well. What Dante told me about stars being our lost loved ones echoes in my head.

I let out a pathetic-sounding snort. Is this the ancient one's way of reminding me of my destiny? Or is it a way for me to connect to the afterlife?

Regardless, I snatch it up with a matching pen above it. My steps falter when I round the corner, and my stomach plummets. Adeline's the one behind the register. Seriously? I roll my eyes up to the sky and debate about putting the notebook back. Too late. Her gaze lands on me.

"Hi, Sierra," she says without the typical bitterness coating it.

"Hey, what are you doing here?" I ask warily. Doesn't she have a group of kids to harass, or babies to steal candy from?

If she senses my apprehension, she doesn't show it. She rocks back and forth on her heel and shrugs.

"I volunteer here a couple of days a week. I mean, what else can we do?"

Her volunteer? I stifle the laugh that threatens to bubble up. Of course, she would, the freaking golden girl of the school.

"It must be boring here, though," I hedge, casting my glance around the empty store.

"It can be; that's why I only do a few hours at a time. It gets me extra credit, though; you should try it."

I'm struggling to figure out if that's a fake smile plastered across her face and she's goading me or not being rude for once. Placing my items on the counter, I decide not to even reply.

"Oooh, I like this one," she says, sliding it over the scanner.

That's it. I can't take it. There's only so much bullshit I can take.

"Why are you being nice to me?" I ask, a hard edge to my voice.

Adeline glances up quickly and frowns, her mask of friendliness slipping. There's the girl I recognize.

"We got off on the wrong foot. I want to start over."

This may be the altered reality. Because the Adeline standing in front of me isn't who I've hated these past several weeks. I eye her cautiously, looking for any hint she's not real. Everything about her seems the same, except her attitude. She's been avoiding me since I sucked the water from her and her friend's bodies. Maybe fear is making her be nice. Self-preservation can be a strong motivator.

"Emma's my best friend. No magic button erases what you did to her, and I won't-"

"I know, and for that, I'm sorry," she cuts me off mid-rant. "I've left her alone, and I'm not asking you to be my friend. Can we agree that we both did wrong and move on?"

What's her angle here? I soften my glare. "Fine. A truce it is."

I hold my hand out to shake on it. All the while, I feel like I'm making a deal with the devil.

CHAPTER 8

Emma

Maverick's been gone a lot lately. His job keeps him busy, but it feels like so much more. It's almost as if he's holding back from fully being in a relationship with me. We kiss and cuddle, and the occasional romp in the sheets, but it's nowhere near what I envisioned living with a partner would be like, even if it's just on the weekends.

I'm a little frustrated after waking up alone for the second day in a row. Sighing, I grab my makeup bag from "my drawer" of the bathroom. I swipe some concealer over the dark half-circles below my eyes and quickly work with my eyeshadow, liner, and mascara. I don't know why I try this hard; Maverick probably won't be home until late again. And by then, most of my makeup will be past its prime.

Since Sierra used her gift against Adeline and her friends, most people have kept their distance from me. Although I still hear the whispered voices calling me blonde spawn. I try my hardest not to let it get to me. But I'll never be their equal; I'll never fit in and be accepted. No matter how hard I try or what I do, it comes down to what makes me *me*.

I shoot a text to Ainsley, letting her know I'm running a few minutes late. Every Sunday morning, we spend a few hours at the Repository researching the transition. We're both on the edge of doing it, but it's terrifying. There's a greater chance of our kind not taking to the immortal ritual and dying in the process. A shudder rolls through me. Sierra told me what it was like for her, and I honestly don't know if I could endure that level of pain.

Tugging the door closed behind me, I hop into Ainsley's little red car, and we head to the large stone building that holds all the answers. There's a small closed-off corner that hardly anybody uses. That's become our spot. I scan the worn editions and find the book I left off with. We never take any books from the library; we don't want to draw attention to what we look up. The Repository isn't on the Guardian Academy's grounds, but I feel it isn't beyond spreading rumors and lies. I've already been at the center of several of those and don't want to give them any ammo to use against me.

"Hey. Check this out," I say, grabbing her attention from the research documents on the table. "They reference a witch, Evie. It says that Evie's helped other half-breeds transition into immortals with an extremely low mortality rate."

"How does she do it?" Ainsley asks, scooting closer to me to look over my shoulder at the scribbled writing in the old book.

The edges are frayed, and it looks like coffee stains dot along the center. The age of this book is unknown; there's no copyright page, and the author isn't even listed.

"The powerful spell caster has a particular regimen she uses to alter the biochemistry right down to the molecule to make the cells adapt to the change," I read the words as a grin spreads across my face. "I think we found it!"

"Where do we find her?"

"It says here that she resides in Pine Valley." I turn toward her, my eyebrows scrunching together. I've never heard of that, but it sounds like a town where a Christmas movie could be filmed. "Where's that?"

Ainsley sighs and throws her head back. "Of course, she would. That's on the other side of the country. It's probably about a four-hour ride, give or take."

"Road trip next Sunday?"

"Sounds like a plan. In the meantime, we should learn everything about this Evie witch."

"I agree." I glance back down to the worn pages and skim across the words, looking for every bit of helpful information and jotting it down in my notebook.

A few hours later, with little information, I stopped by the grocery store on my way back to Maverick's place to pick up dinner. Meatloaf, oven-roasted corn on the cob, and sweet potato fries are the best. It's an odd combination, but it's his favorite.

The clock on the wall shows nearly eight o'clock at night before I finally hear keys turning at the front door. My racing pulse slows, knowing he's safe at home again. Each day seems like a sick, twisted game of Russian roulette, with his life on the line. Running up to him, I wrap my arms around him and inhale his signature musky scent.

His arm glides around my waist before tilting his head down to place a chaste kiss on my lips. He pulls away before I even get a chance to kiss him back.

"Long day?" I ask.

"Never-ending. That vampire bar I told you about is just the beginning; there's a whole string of them across the United States."

What would drive a human to want the blood sucked out of them is beyond me. No matter what they promise you.

"Ew. Of course, there would be." I shake my head. "Are you hungry? I made your favorite."

He nods and stalks toward the kitchen. A weird energy is coming off of him tonight that makes me feel like I'm walking on eggshells. Standing a short distance from him, I watch as he tugs the strap of his bow off and sets it against the wall, followed by his tactical belt, heavy with other weapons that he lays on the small stand between the living room and the kitchen. Then takes off toward the bathroom.

Luckily, the food wasn't done cooking until about a half hour ago, and I could keep them warm in the oven. Plating out the dishes, I set his plate down on one side of the table and take the seat across from it. Maverick returns from the bathroom and sits, his eyes never landing on mine. I know because I've been watching his every movement since he got home.

After forking some meatloaf into his mouth, he says, "Wow, this is really good."

My mom was an excellent cook and taught me the best way to a man's heart is through his stomach. Longing grips me like a vise. I know she did wrong by staying with my father. But did she deserve to be thrown in jail? Other than being the one to draw the prisoner's blood, she didn't do anything wrong as far as I know anyway. I miss her. I hate that I do, but I can't help it. It's been months since I've seen her.

"Thank you," I reply quietly.

Once dinner's finished and Maverick grabs my plate and heads toward the sink to wash them, I finally dare to ask him what's been plaguing me these last few nights. Resting my palm on his bicep, I wait until he turns toward me. The heat from his skin warms my fingers, and I can feel his muscles tense below them.

"Mav," I whisper. "Why does it feel like you're pulling away from me?"

He tenses and lets out a slow breath that tickles my forehead. "Don't do this, Emma."

My eyebrows bunch together in confusion. "Don't do what?"

His eyes soften. "I don't want to hurt you."

Alarm bells start going off in my head. What has he done that he thinks will hurt me?

"Are you cheating on me?" I blurt the first thing that comes to mind. My voice raises along with the panicked hairs on the back of my neck.

"What? No, I'd never do that," he says quickly, running his fingers down the side of my face.

"Then what's gotten into you the past two weeks? You're never around anymore. When you are?" I shrug. "It's been different."

"I'm doing my best," he snaps.

"Best at what, pushing me away? I love you, Mav, and I'm giving you everything I have, but you're holding back," I spit.

He blinks and freezes. That's the first time I've dropped the l-bomb on him. We've never told each other we loved one another, but I felt it.

Regaining his composure, he says quietly, "I can't allow myself to love somebody that hard and only temporarily."

I wince, and the breath whooshes out of me as if I just took a blow to the chest. Temporary. He thinks this is temporary? But why? Tears sting at my eyes, and I already know the truth in his words.

I'm not enough. I'll never be enough for him, will I?

His warm hazel eyes search my face. "I just can't stand the thought of losing you," he says in a tight voice.

"So, you're dumping me because you don't want to lose me? What kind of backward logic is that?"

"I never said I was breaking up with you, but I can't watch you grow old and die while I continue living. I've seen it before, and I can't do it."

As if his words were his treasured blue and silver arrows piercing through my heart, the pain of knowing he doesn't even accept me for being a half-breed fills my heart with nothing but unimaginable agony. I thought he loved me for who I was. Man, was I ever wrong. I thought he was different.

"What have we been doing then?" My voice cracks as I try to hold the emotion back, but it's like a tidal wave coming in, wave by wave, each one much worse than the last; it's only a matter of time before the tide consumes me. He stands quietly in front of me, an unreadable mask in place.

"Are you saying we wouldn't be having this conversation if I were an immortal like you?" I add bitterly.

Nothing but more silence. The soft sound of the bubbles popping in the dishwater reaches me.

"You think it's easy for me to know what your job entails? That literally every single day that I say goodbye to you, it could be the final time," I spit the words at him with venom. How dare he think that I don't live with the same fear? The only difference is he's the one going out there every day and putting his life at risk, while I'm merely existing in his. "Well, guess what? This is the final time. Goodbye, Maverick."

I spin on my heels and dash to the bedroom, grab my duffle bag from the closet and yank the bureau drawers open so hard they let out a squeak. Tears blur my vision as I fist my clothes and shove them into the bag.

I can't believe I fell for him, hook, line, and sinker. Footsteps sound behind me, and my already tense body tightens even more. He stands just behind me; the heat of his body tells me so. I hate how my body reacts to his. It always seems to know when he's close.

"Emma," he breathes. "Stop. Please."

"No," I shout, twisting my body toward him. I jab my pointer into his breastbone until my finger bends with the pressure. "You're a coward," I sob. "Each day you walk out that door could be the last time I see you, yet I'm here. I'm willing to risk losing you one day because I love you so goddamn much, but you can't see past the fact that I'm not an immortal."

His eyes narrow, and his palms grip my biceps, hard but not painful. "You're right; I am a coward when it comes to you."

"Glad we cleared that up," I huff. "Now, leave me alone so I can pack, and you'll never have to see me again." I try to turn in his grasp, but it's useless; his hands are like an iron fist holding me in place.

"You're not going anywhere," he whispers, stepping closer until I feel his haggard breath on my skin. He releases his grip on my arms to cradle my head and neck, forcing me to look into those fierce hazel eyes. Maverick's lips part. "I've tried to fight it. I thought I could be stronger than the bond. That if I didn't acknowledge it, the link would fade."

My heart races, thrumming a pulsing beat through my veins like a jackhammer. I whisper harshly, "What are you talking about, Mav?"

"Loving you in one human lifetime will never be enough. You're my anima gemelli, Emma. My bonded mate." His eyes close tightly, and a frown mars his handsome face. "When you die, I'll become a wanderer; my soul will search the universe to find you. A part of me that will never be whole again." He takes in a haggard breath. "You'll destroy me," he says in anguish as he places his forehead against mine.

Tears cascade down my cheeks, forming a river of heat and salt. I knew it felt different with him ever since the beginning. I thought it was just my heart's way of getting me through the hell of these last several months. But all along, he's been the one. Right here in front of me, it's always been him.

"Then, I guess we'll destroy each other because I can't fathom a life without you, Maverick. I either want all of you or nothing. I can't go halfway. If what you're saying is true? It's fate. Who are we to ignore fate?" I say quietly before crashing my lips against his and pouring all my desperation into it.

He kisses me back as if this were the last time we'd ever be together.

Each day isn't promised to us; it's a gift. It's about time we understood that. I know what I need to do. I know my fate; I feel it deep in my bones. There's only one way to fully be his equal.

One path to my family's redemption.

Ruby

The urge to get new ink has been clawing at me for ages. Well, my last was the Phoenix a handful of months ago. That doesn't stop me from needing more. Tugging the smooth benitoite portal stone out of my back pocket, I point at a random wall in my apartment. The gray of the wall turns to a smokey hue and dances with other shades of colors until Alex's front door reveals itself on the other side.

Stepping through and closing my hands together, I tuck the stone back into my pants. Knock. Knock. I wait for several seconds while I hear muffled footsteps through the door. Alex didn't know I was coming, so hopefully, I'm not intruding.

The door opens wide, and Alex's striking amber eyes take me in. "Well, look at who decided to stop by," he mumbles.

"Oh shut it, you big smelly dog," I balk and come in for a hug. Alex wraps me in those thick arms as he kicks the door closed. "Am I interrupting anything?"

He releases me. "No. Not at all. After the last phone call, I figured you'd be coming by soon anyway."

Right. I told him about Eric and some of the fucked up feelings I've been having. My mind has been a clusterfuck lately.

"I could use a release." That's the understatement of the year. I could go for a vacation to a private island surrounded by nothing but the sounds of the forest, no human or supernatural contact whatsoever, someplace like this house.

"What did you have in mind?" He walks in front of me, leading me to his back room, where his tattoo studio resides.

His broad shoulders nearly touch both sides of the hall. The floor-to-ceiling windows let the natural light in through the whole house. Alex lives out in the middle of the forest in Oregon. He's a beta wolf, so he has to stay somewhat close to his tribe, but he's far enough away that we don't have to worry about me being spotted here. Tensions are still high amongst our kinds.

To be honest, at this point, I don't even care what he creates. I just need the sting of the needle against my skin. Then it comes to me, and I speak without thinking, "I want a skeleton holding a black rose. With a ruby ring on her finger."

"Ah. The beautiful jacket a certain someone gave you." He says in a taunting way. Mischief lights up his face.

"It's a beautiful piece," I reply flatly, trying to dissuade any further conversation on the matter.

"I have no doubt," he says as he gathers the necessary equipment. Lining up small plastic cups and splitting open a new needle to put into the tattoo gun. Alex pats the chair. "Hop on up."

I do as instructed. The machine hasn't even punctured my skin, and I can already feel the calming effects it has on me. Maybe the chair's embedded with calming energy.

"Where do you want her?" He spritzes some rubbing alcohol on a paper towel.

I bite my lip as I think. "How about over my heart?"

His eyes flick to mine. "Are you sure?"

"Yeah. I don't have much room elsewhere for a piece like this, and I think it captures who I am." Even I can tell I'm rambling.

I don't want to admit out loud the depths of my feelings for Eric. I'm terrified of them and what they could mean.

"Okay. Off with the shirt, then." He gestures with his hand.

I've taken my clothes off in front of Alex more times than I can count. It doesn't bother me in the least. And it helps that he's not a perv about it. Left in just leggings and a bra, the plastic-like feeling of the chair sticks to my skin. Leaning back against the headrest, I slow my breathing as Alex lightly outlines with a felt tip marker. Mostly, all of his artwork is done freehand.

"So. Are you going to tell me the real reason you want this or what?" his deep voice breaks the quiet.

"Like I said. It captures who I am perfectly." He doesn't need to know more than that. His yellowish eyes hold mine for a moment before he lets out a soft sigh.

After several minutes filled with the sound of light rain tapping on the glass window behind us, he hands me a mirror. "What do you think?"

Right now, it's just a flat outline, but it shows the hand of the skeleton bringing the rose up to her face to smell it. It's eery how close it resembles the one Eric had custom made for me.

"It's perfect," I admit.

"Any changes?" he asks, fiddling with the buttons on his machine.

"Nope. Do your thing, cowboy." I grin up at him.

Alex shakes his head and scowls. "Only you can get away with abusing me this way."

He fires up his trusty machine and traces all the lines he drew. I already feel the uneasiness seeping out of my body. The sharp bite of the needle feels good. If I could capture what it feels like and sell it, I'd be the wealthiest woman in the world. I can't be the only person who feels immense freedom as the biting machine tears through my skin and lets out all the darkness trapped within the layers.

"I gotta ask you something, Ruby." He doesn't look up from his work. His hand continues to drag the needle over my skin while his other hand wipes away the excess ink with a damp cloth.

"Yeah?" I ask warily, his serious tone setting me slightly on edge.

"What if he's the mate you were destined for?" His husky baritone feels too loud in this room.

The word mate seems to reverberate off the walls. Echoing in the distance. Among werewolves and other shifter species, they have mates, which is very similar to our kind having an anima gemella—an eternal soul mate.

"You know I don't really believe that shit," I scoff. How can you be paired with one individual for your whole existence? Especially for species that can live for thousands of years. It doesn't make sense to me.

"But you've seen what happens to others when their soul mate perishes."

I'd rather not be reminded of the wanderers. "You can also die of a broken heart."

"I'm just saying, maybe you should give him a chance." The tattoo gun lifts from my skin, and he sighs. A frown cuts across that handsome face, and his yellow eyes narrow on me.

"If that were the case, and Eric is my anima gemella, I would've felt it right off. From what I've been taught, the bond would be undeniable."

Alex shakes his head before wiping my skin again. The needle bumps along my skin in a trail I can't see but can feel deep down. I would know, right? If he were my fated soul mate? Shit, now Alex has me questioning everything I've ever known.

God damn him!

"But you said so yourself; there's something different about him." He pauses and pulls the tattoo gun away to dip it into the ink. "Maybe the frozen heart of the ice queen is finally thawing."

I punch him hard in the shoulder. "Shut up."

He flashes me a wicked grin. "Come on, Ms. *Hart*, you know it's true."

I love how he emphasized my last name, not. "Just do what I'm paying you to do," I snip at him and fight the urge to cross my arms over my chest. All that would do is serve to be in his way and smear the ink across my chest.

"Ha," he barks a hearty laugh and grabs more ink. "You're not paying me for shit."

"I'm paying you by gracing you with my presence." I smile coyly at him and flutter my lashes.

"Oh jeez, like I haven't heard that one before," he says but gets back to work on my skin.

I close my eyes and relish the feeling of bliss. However temporary the effects are, this is what grounds me. This reminds me to keep breathing, fighting, and living.

Sometimes, in the world that we live in, we need these little moments that seem so insignificant but, in fact, shape us in ways we don't quite understand. Take our friendship, for example. Alex is a shifter, and I'm an immortal guardian sworn to protect humans from his kind. And yet he's my best friend, the most trusted person in my life, but we're supposed to be sworn enemies. We're raised in communities that hate and fear the others.

Graystone needs to come out of the dark ages and change with the times. We all deserve to live in a world that accepts us, flaws and all. Nilo started the change, but I'll push him harder than ever to make this world what I know it can be.

After some time, Alex sets the tattoo gun down and gives my skin a final swipe with rubbing alcohol. Reaching for the mirror on his desk, he tells me, "She's a little puffy like you on the days you don't get your beauty rest, but I think once the redness settles, she'll look awesome."

I gaze into the reflective glass at my new artwork and smile at the master tattooer. "She's perfect. Thank you!"

"You're welcome," he pauses awkwardly. "If I was in your shoes and there was even a remote chance that Eric's your mate, I'd break down every barrier to let him in. You can't live a good life always battling the scars of the past. It's about time you put a new canvas up and let him paint you a love story you can't refuse. What do you have to lose?"

CHAPTER 9

Sierra

Mom's making blueberry pancakes again for the boy; I still don't know his name. I don't know which version is reality, here with my mother and child or at the Guardian Academy. I'm too afraid to ask; I finally have my mom back. What if it's not real? Or what if this version of me is real, and I don't even know who I am?

I thought I was living a lie before, not knowing I was immortal. But now I don't know anything. What if they're both real? Could there be multiple dimensions in which I live? Each time I go to sleep, I wake up in the other world. Either I have Dante and Emma, or I have my mom and child. There's no in-between, and I don't want to lose either. I can't lose her again.

I look over at the toddler and admire how much he looks like Dante. The chocolate brown hair and facial features are barely hidden behind the chubby cheeks. There's no doubt whose son he is. An ache blooms across my chest. I can't feel the connection to Dante, and that terrifies me. He's my anima gemella; I should always be able to feel him through our shared bond. But I don't when I'm here with my mom and child.

I jolt upright and gasp for breath. Suddenly, I'm back in the dorm room at the academy. My breathing is labored, and my pulse pounds steadily in my temple. Glancing over to Emma's bed, I find her staring directly at me.

"Bad dream, again?" she whispers.

How can I tell her the truth that I don't even know if it's a dream or if it's real? "You could say that." I rub the sleep out of my blurry eyes and try to focus on the digital clock on my bedside: four o'clock in the morning.

Reaching my hands underneath my pillow, I grab my journal and try to jot down every single detail of the "dream" I just had before I lose it. That's the way it goes, though; within several minutes of waking up, I can barely remember what happened. It's so strange.

One lone tear leaks out of the corner of my eye as the sadness comes back in full force. In this world, my mother's dead, and my son doesn't exist. But I can feel my bond with Dante like a heartbeat in my veins, strong and steady. Tucking the journal back under the pillow, I swing my legs out and stretch.

"Where are you going?" Emma asks as I begin rummaging through my bureau and pull out a pair of black joggers.

"I'm going for a run." Slipping into the pants, I tug my hair into a loose ponytail.

She yawns. "At this hour?"

"I don't want to fall back asleep." There's too much that haunts me when I'm not awake.

Quietly shutting the door behind me, I slip down the stairs and out of the building without anybody noticing me. I tug my cell phone out of the side pocket and open the app that I found that plays calming sounds. Clicking on the thunderstorm one, I let the soft rumbles of thunder drown out the chaos threatening my sanity. My feet begin to pound the asphalt below me.

Without thinking about where I'm headed, I find myself at the cemetery, and a sharp inhale reminds me of who lies behind that small iron fence. The gate creaks as I push it open and latch it. I know this path like the lines in my palm; I can walk it with my eyes closed. My steps slow as I near the back half where my mother's grave resides. Lowering myself to the ground, I begin picking out the small weeds that managed to grow since the last time I was here.

I come often enough that the grass below me never really perks up. It's always squished down like a bed from a fawn lying beside her mother. My fingers trace the outline of her name etched into the stone, and a small sob rakes itself free.

"I wish you were here. You'd know what to do." Tears stream down my face in waves. Closing my eyes, I picture her standing over the stove making her grandson pancakes. That's the only image that stays in my mind, the main thing I remember from those dreams.

"Is it really you on the other side? Please, Mom, give me some sign that it's real."

My chest tightens as I wait for anything to tell me she hears me. Nothing happens. It's a struggle to push my lungs to expand enough to take a breath in. What did I expect, for her to materialize right before my eyes? I begin to cry again and lay beside where her body is directly below me.

"I can't keep going like this, Mom. I'm exhausted and feel like I've lost my way. I no longer know what's real or fake or who to trust. I feel like you're trying to reach out to me from the afterlife. You really need to tell me what to do here because I just feel like I'm failing at everything."

At some point, I must've fallen asleep because when my heavy lids open again, the sun is high in the sky and beating down on me, and the skin on my face is warm.

"Shit," I exclaim, jumping up and brushing the dirt off my clothes. I'm late for classes. My feet pound into the road below me, taking me farther and farther from any answers I desperately need.

Also, I don't need another tardy slip Matias sees. I'm already on thin ice with him; this won't help my case. Dashing to the dorm to grab my bag, I slip through the door of the chemistry class and mouth the words; I'm sorry to the male teacher sitting behind his desk. His eyebrows raise, and he points to my empty seat.

Just great. I ignore the stares from the other classmates and the hushed mumbles and snickers they let out. Screw them all. They have no idea what it's like to be me right now. None of them have had to battle villains as I have. The professor drones on about this chemical reaction and what it will do if you don't handle it properly. When will I ever really use this? Probably never.

My notebook sits open on my desk, still a blank page, when the bell rings. I can feel Professor Evander's eyes on me as I shove the notebook into my backpack. Slinging it over my shoulder as I stand, he stops me by calling my name once I'm close to the door.

"Where were you that was more important than being here in class?"

"I'm sorry."

An expectant look crosses his face. "Where were you?" he repeats.

I avert my eyes and whisper, "The cemetery."

"Oh." His facial features morph from stern to sorrowful. "Don't be late again, okay?"

I nod my understanding and walk out before looking back at him again. He wears a worried expression. I only have one class to sit through: combat training. Once I blast through that one, I'll be off to my magic training with Professor Zuri.

The bell finally rings, signaling the end of the school day. Shoving my notebook in my backpack, I sling it over my shoulder. The hall's a sea of students as I approach the back exit. I meet with Yuri on Tuesdays and Thursdays to enhance my gift. It's the only time I'm allowed to take the iron bracelets off while on school grounds. As I push through the metal door, the sunlight beams down around me, and a soft wind blows my hair across my face.

Pausing just past the threshold, I tug a hair tie off my wrist and sweep my hair into a high ponytail. The back lawn is surprisingly empty; usually, on nice days like today, students will be milling about. Once I reach the back fence, I hop over it easily and trudge through the small winding path into the forest. Since my magic was labeled as destructive, I have to train even farther away from others.

The trees thin out and reveal a clearing of about two acres or so of tall grasses and weeds. Some wildflowers are freckled in here and there. Yuri probably won't arrive for several minutes, so I toss my bag on the ground and lean up against the base of a large oak tree.

I rest my eyes and try to meditate like she taught me. My hands rest on my thighs, and I breathe in slowly through my nose and out my mouth, counting to three on every inhale and exhale. I focus on each and every body part, from my toes softly grazing the grass to my back, which is still tense, and finally, to a face that can feel the soft breeze like a whisper. I push out all thoughts and feelings from my mind as I relax deeper into the tree.

"God, my mind's a jumbled mess lately," I huff out when trying to push them all out doesn't work.

The sound of footsteps in the distance pulls me from my thoughts. Yuri's silvery hair bobs above the tall weeds until her face and torso come into view. Her navy cardigan and linen pants seem so out of place in the woods.

Nodding to me as I stand, she asks, "Meditating?"

"Trying to. I'm afraid it looks easier than it is sometimes," I admit.

"It takes a lot of practice to gain power over oneself, but once you do? It's like opening a door to another realm."

I don't know about another realm, but sometimes it would be nice to keep my mind quiet. I hold my wrists out to her to remove the bracelets. I never take them off myself, just in case. I am technically still on school grounds. Tucking them in the pockets of her loose-legged pants, I await her instructions.

"We've worked on ways to use your gift for good through gardening, cleaning, and averting flood waters." She brushes off some fuzz from the towering dandelions that freckle the field. "Today, we're going to use it as a weapon."

My eyes flash up to hers as the muscles in my body tense with apprehension. "Why?"

"Because Sierra, I know the ancient ones gave this gift to you for a reason, and it's not to be a rainmaker."

"What about headmaster Matias?" I cross my arms, not liking where this is going.

"What of him?"

"He said it's too powerful and uncontrolled, and he did this for the safety of all the students," I reply. These words have been a constant in my mind since I got suspended.

"I see," she says softly. "Can I be blunt with you, Ms. Walker?"

"Of course."

"Elementals are very rare in our kind. You are the first in centuries to be gifted with an elemental power. That means something's coming."

"But I already defeated him. He's locked away. The prophecy's been fulfilled."

"Yes, it would seem it has, but prophecies can change, just like our futures. Every action changes the projected outcome. I can feel it, Sierra. Call it a sixth sense, if you will. Soul seers have been blindsided before, and it would be unwise of us not to utilize the time we have to sharpen all of our skills."

A shudder ripples through me at her statements. Dante said something similar. "What do you suggest we do?"

"You've made spears of ice you can chuck, but how about a bullet made of ice?"

"The closest to that would be the small hail when I make a massive storm."

"Yes, that would be perfect. Instead of hell-fire, we'll unleash frost-fire. Start by making ice in the shape of a bullet."

Holding my hands out in front of me, I picture what she said. Coldness seeps over me as the tiny shard of ice begins to form. Changing the shape from a ball to a bullet with a sharp tip is like molding it out of hard clay.

Meeting her gaze, she says, "Keep going. Make several more until they're all suspended in the air."

I shape each tiny block of ice one by one. Sweat beads on my lip even though I'm surrounded by ice. About 30 frozen bullets are circling me when she tells me to stop.

"Now fling them all toward that tree." She points to the edge of the clearing where another big oak stands tall. The branches up above make a massive canopy.

Bracing my feet against the ground, I wave my hands in front of me until all the bullets are in one small area close to my chest. I forcefully push my hands out as if shoving at a wall. The ice flies through the air and strikes the tree with a loud thwack. Chunks of bark explode around it, some landing about ten feet from the base. We cross the distance to look at the damage, the tall grass tickles my calves. Small holes go all the way through the tree and are scattered throughout where it hit.

"Oh my god." I cover my mouth with my trembling fingertips as bile burns the back of my throat. "That can kill someone," I whisper.

"That was the intention. You did it perfectly." She rests her hand on my shoulder as I try to pry my eyes from the damage I inflicted. "If you're out in the field fighting dark ones, for instance, the sooner you dispatch them, the better. Speed is everything in battle, Sierra."

"And what if I mess up and hit the wrong person?"

"That's why we practice to ensure you're ready." Yuri turns and walks back to where we were standing. "Now, do it again. But this time, make a hundred."

And so I do. On the fourth try, the tips of my fingers form icicles. Then, each one after that, the coldness travels up my hands, leaving small ice crystals in their wake. My eyes sting as a pounding force begins in the back of my head. Tuning out everything and everyone, I create a wall of ice bullets in front of me that is so thick I no longer see the target about forty feet away.

Gathering my strength, I push hard against it. A groan escapes my mouth when I send the weapon coasting across the field. On impact, the tree explodes with a deafening crack, throwing branches and leaves high up into the air before crashing down. All that remains is a jagged base that looks like something out of a haunted forest movie.

Frost coats my hands, but I barely notice the biting cold as I sit on a stump to catch my breath. I never knew the amount of damage ice can cause. It makes me wonder what else I can make. Sweat coats the hair above my forehead in sharp contrast to my frozen hands.

I twist my hands to form another shard of ice, but nothing comes. Each hail storm of bullets I made drained me little by little until the last batch took everything I had left. It'll take time for my gift to regain strength, and I can wield it again.

"Astonishing," Yuri's voice drifts over to me as she inspects the tree, running her hands down the scarified bark. "Simply unbelievable."

Dante

"**Y**ou're sure this will work?" I hate asking Konstantina for confirmation. She's a great witch, but there's too much on the line if I fail. Far too many innocent children are at risk.

"Yes, Dante. This isn't the first time I've done a mimicking spell, you know." She hands over the small vial with shimmering blue liquid in it. The particles sparkle like glitter in the early morning rays. "It's fast-acting and won't be able to mask you for long."

"How long do I have?"

"About an hour, I'd say."

"That's good enough, thanks." I put the potion into a small pocket in my bag to use once I'm ready.

"My pleasure."

Konstantina's been helping out at the Alchemist's Palace in town. It turns out Maggie's not that great at crafting potions, and her father asked Konstantina to step in while Maggie's away training with a distant relative. The bell over the door chimes, alerting her of a new customer.

"Just remember, one slip will blow the cover."

"Understood."

Nodding to the young lady that came in, I step through the front door and pull out my blue benitoite portal stone. Sighing, I picture the elementary school that's my target. The smoke swirls around before revealing a blue-brick building surrounded by a chain-linked fence. If only that little scrap of metal could keep the real monsters out.

I'm hunting a Mormo, a ghost-like demon cursed to only survive by devouring small children. They are the most wicked of the demon species, in my opinion. Three children have disappeared in a span of five days from this school. Our sources say the demon targeted another school not far from here. Unfortunately, by the time the immortal guardians arrived, the Mormo had already disappeared.

Twisting the top off the vial, I throw it back and swallow the bitter-tasting liquid. I shiver as the feeling of spiders crawls across my skin, changing my appearance to resemble a young boy, ripe for the picking.

I easily hop over that measly fence and spot several children playing on the playground.

"Hi, I'm Dante!" I tell the boy closest to me.

He's probably around eight or so, with wild brown hair. I haven't been a kid in so long; how do they even talk now? So many of them are glued to screens, that I'm surprised they can even communicate with one another.

"I'm Mack. Are you new?" he asks in a small voice as he looks behind me.

"Yeah," I answer, focusing my mind on his to compel him. "Have you heard about the kids that were taken?"

"Y-yes," he stammers. "They were over there talking to the lady that smells funny." He points a chubby little finger to the other side of the grounds, where the fence butts up against the side of the forest.

It's a perfect hiding place for a demon.

"What do you know about the smelly lady?"

"She asks us if we want to play with her!" he exclaims. Then, he frowns, looks down, and kicks at the dirt. "She said her kids died."

I close my eyes briefly and wonder how many children she was able to lure to their deaths by saying that. How many good, innocent children were only trying to help her?

"What else do you know about her?" I coax.

"None of the adults listen! We've told them she needs help, that she needs a bath, but they don't smell her or hear her." He throws his little hands up in the air.

"Okay, buddy, thank you for all the help. Tell all your friends never to go near her, and you stay close to the teachers, okay?"

"Okay," he answers before he scrambles off toward the other students.

Disappearing around the building, I pull my cell phone out and text Nathaniel.

"Call in the lockdown; I have what I need."

Momentarily, an alarm blares out of the loudspeakers on the edges of the building. It instructs all the school staff that there's an active threat and to shelter inside. Chaos ensues as the teachers scramble to get all the kids back inside. Luckily, the ones out here are still young enough that they don't quite understand that this isn't just a drill. Once there's nothing but silence outside, I jog toward the spot Mack indicated and chuck my backpack on the ground.

I don't have much time left for this potion, so I have to work quickly. I won't be able to catch the Mormo unless she thinks I'm a child. She's able to cloak herself from anything and everybody unless their innocence calls to her. The child must willingly take her hand for her to be able to feed off them. They're known to find a dark hiding place to hide their terrifying features and trick the kids into grabbing their hands.

If a child was to see a Mormo, I'm sure they'd turn and run away. The body is wraithlike in its wispy form like smoke, with a mouth lined with several rows of sharp teeth like a Great White shark. Large bat-like ears come to a pointed tip, and finally, blind eyes that are creamy-white with no pupils.

I tug the bottle of vanishing ink from my bag and quickly draw a pentagram in the grass close to the opening in the fence. It doesn't matter that the Mormo can't see the ink; it just so happens to be the one I like to carry on me. When you fight demons that can see, they'll fight with everything they have to escape a trap.

"Is someone there?" a whispered voice reaches me.

"I'm Dante. Who are you?" I reply while silently drawing my katana from the scabbard on my back.

"My name's Amalia. It seems I'm tangled in these vines. Can you help me get free?" the Mormo asks in a sing-song voice.

"Sure," I answer, stepping closer.

A frail-looking hand slowly reaches through the broken metal fence.

"Just take my hand, child."

I plant my feet firmly on the ground and take in a steady breath before clasping her hand. Ice shoots up my veins from the tips of my fingers all the way to my shoulder and down to my toes. The demon begins to tug me closer, but I yank her hand back toward me. With enough force, she hits the fence. She shrieks loudly, her voice echoing across the silent playground.

"I'm trying to help you get out of those vines." A sly grin spreads across my face as the Mormo struggles to free her hand from my grasp.

Tugging on the demon's hand again to pull her through the opening isn't as easy as I thought it'd be. This one's strong and fights back with vigor. Sheathing my katana, I grasp her forearm in my other hand and pull with every bit of strength I can muster.

The Mormo comes crashing through the fence and lands with a thud on the ground. A morbid necklace made of tiny finger bones and wire wrap around the neck multiple times. Each small bone is a trophy from a kill that rattles a hollow sound with every movement.

"A guardian," she spits the words at me like acid. Her white eyes narrow.

Even though they're blind, they have excellent senses. She continues to try to break free as I drag her closer and closer to the pentagram. The coldness comes over me like a wet blanket. Like a viper, she strikes and clamps onto my left arm with razor-sharp teeth—pain lances across my skin like an inferno.

"Damn it!" I ground out while letting go of her with my right arm to grab the dagger at my belt.

All of my weapons are infused with demon-killing magic. Although the katana's always my first choice, it isn't feasible in close combat like this. The blade glides through the air as I slam the sharp point into the back of the beast's neck.

It cries out again but removes its teeth from my flesh. The cold air stings as it comes in contact with the open wound, and I grind my teeth together as I force myself not to let her go. She jostles herself around, struggling to free herself.

"I can smell your mate on your skin as if the scent is a living being. I will hunt her next guardian," she snarls as inky black blood drips to the grassy ground.

"I won't give you that chance. You're not walking away from this. And since you threaten my anima gemelli," I growl, tugging her closer to my face until I can feel her hot, wretched breath fan across my chin. "I will make the end of your existence long and painful."

The Mormo tries to dart away, dragging me farther from the pentagram. Digging my heels into the sod, I wait until her arm has some slack and yank her toward my body while I twist around and cage the demon's back to my chest. Her long fingernails claw at my arms and tear at my skin until her nails puncture it deep enough that I can feel it scrape against my bones. Finally, to the edge, I thrust the demon into the invisible barrier, letting go of it altogether and stepping just out of reach.

Dark crimson drips steadily from the wounds on my arms. I'm not too worried about it. They'll heal, but man, does it hurt like hell. I flex my fist a few times and stretch out my arms to ensure I can still utilize my strength. An animalistic growl escapes my throat when I realize there's not enough strength to be able to torture this demon for as long as I want to. I'll need to take a healing elixir quickly to ensure no lasting effects from the demon's poisonous ichor. Any bite or scratch can turn septic; it's one of an immortal's few weaknesses.

The Mormo charges at me but slams against the invisible wall. She bares her numerous teeth as spit flies from her gaping mouth. Flexing my fist again only makes a white-hot pain emerge. I could just banish the demon to the realms of hell. Threatening Sierra ruined any shot of this demon surviving this. The sword makes a soft whooshing noise as I pull it out and hold it before me.

An image of this entire playground littered with the blood and bodies of innocent children haunts my vision—one for each bone around the demon's neck. The sight repulses me as I silently take in the countless trophies she's acquired.

"How many innocent children have you murdered?" I snarl.

"Not enough," she says in that sweet voice meant to lure the children in.

I swing my blade through the air, and the demon throws her hands in front of her face, hearing the air whoosh between us. My katana slices through the underside of her forearm, spilling more of the black liquid that runs in the demon's veins. It shrieks and jumps back, only to be met with another barrier. I swing again and again as the monster shrieks until nothing but slits dot along her arms and legs like a twisted version of a hasselback potato.

Sweat beads on my forehead and slides down my face as I regain strength. The wounds on my own arms scream in agony as the trickle continues to flow. A mixture of both mine and the demon's blood seeps into the ground below. I'd never be able to shed enough blood to give the victims the justice they deserve. All I can do is vow to stop it from continuing.

"You will never harm another child in this world, for with my final blow, I banish your existence from this realm," I shout the incantation.

One last well-placed swing and the head of the Mormo is cut clean off and falls to the ground, followed by the body crumpling into itself. The eery white eyes are wide open, and the mouth is twisted in pain as the remains begin to smoke and disappear. After a few short moments, all that's left are the bones of the innocents.

I snatch them up and place them in my bag. The Guard can identify the victims by the DNA within the bones, and from there, we can give their families closure. At least if they know their child has been found deceased, they can start the grieving process. It's not much, but they won't continue searching for something they'll never find.

CHAPTER 10

Sierra

It's surreal to be sitting cross-legged on the sofa beside my mom, watching soap operas. My son sits on the rug below us, smashing giant building blocks together. I have no idea what he's making, but he's clearly convinced he's following some blueprint.

"Eat up, dear. Raiden needs you to be strong," my mom coaxes.

"Who?" I turn toward her, confused.

Her eyes hold mine for several seconds as creases form across her forehead. My mom blinks as if in a trance and then gasps, bringing her hand to cover her mouth.

"Oh my." She pauses. "Raiden, my beautiful grandson sweetheart."

I close my eyes tightly and rub at my forehead as another migraine comes on. Of course, that would be his name. Named after the God of thunder and lightning. How could I forget that? What kind of mother forgets what she named her son?

A cold sweat breaks out across my skin, and my stomach sours. My lunch no longer holds any appeal. When will this end?

"I think these episodes are getting worse, Sierra. Are you sleeping enough?" She scoots closer to me on the couch and rubs my back in a circular motion.

"Yes, Mom, I am," I groan, then decide to add, "It feels like that's all I do is sleep."

Her face tightens, and her lips have a grim twist as if she doesn't believe me.

"Would it be better if I take Raiden for a few days back to my house, then you can rest?"

"No!" I answer too quickly. The thought of not seeing them for days floods me with anxiety. "I mean, no, that's not necessary. I want you both here."

I jolt awake with my heart pounding in my throat and taking in huge gulps of air. Turning my face to the side, I see Dante's emerald green irises staring back at me. I take in the room, close my eyes tightly, and work on slowing my breathing.

"Good morning, beautiful," he says in that husky morning voice I love so much.

Scrubbing at my face doesn't help much to clear the fog. I don't usually have those dreams unless I'm at the academy. Come to think of it, this is the first time I've had one next to Dante. Usually, he's my safe space.

"Good morning, handsome," I reply with a scratchy throat.

Opening my eyes and twisting toward the sound of his voice, his face morphs into my son. Raiden, I remember. I close my lids again and rub at them. When I open them again, I see just Dante's face.

His eyebrows draw together, and he tilts his head. "Are you okay?"

"Yeah. Just a weird dream," I reply.

"Wanna talk about it?"

"Not really. I just want to lay here in your arms for a bit longer."

His palm rubs up and down my back. "I'll never say no to that."

I try to recall last night but it's all just a blur. It's like my whole life at this point is the inside of a portal, just swirling around and around. I don't even know what day it is, other than a weekend day. Otherwise, I wouldn't be here with Dante. Even though I hate being separated from him throughout the week, I couldn't imagine Emma being alone in our dorm.

"You don't have to work today?" I ask him.

"Nope. I'm all yours." He gives me a warm smile that reaches his eyes.

"Good," I admit. "It's been a while since it's just been us together."

"I know." He sighs. "I've told you before I'll cut back my hours-"

"No," I cut him off. "You go stir crazy when you're not working." I smirk at him.

"I can find other ways to keep me busy." He wiggles his eyebrows up and down suggestively and kisses my neck.

"I know how much your duty means to you and makes you happy. I'd never ask you to do that." I won't let that heated look distract me from this.

"It wouldn't be a choice, Sierra. In every scenario, I'd choose you."

My heart seems to freeze before it remembers to beat again. His unwavering loyalty never ceases to amaze me.

"And I love you for that, I do." I kiss him deeply, feeling the dream slip farther and farther from my grasp. "I'd never ask that of you. I'm okay with the way things are. I'm busy all week at the academy and training anyway. So, you might as well do something with yourself." I giggle at the feigned hurt look he gives me.

"How are things going with your extra lessons?"

"Honestly? Exhausting." I stifle a yawn, which only proves my point. "I usually meet with Audrey every Monday, Wednesday, and Friday. Then, I train with Yuri on Tuesday and Thursday. It's like I recover from one just to deplete my energy on the next."

Wrinkles form around his eyes as his eyebrows bunch together. "If you need to slow down, tell them."

"I'm okay, I mean it. I need to catch up with everyone else, and Yuri is actually really helpful." I didn't think so initially, but the older professor has grown on me. I think she was feeling me out at first.

"Really?"

I nod. "She helped me to make frost fire."

"Frost fire?" His gaze sweeps over my face.

"A hailstorm of bullets made out of ice," I tell him, grinning.

"Damn." His eyes widen before he grins back. "That's something I've never heard of."

"Yeah. She comes up with many things I never would've thought of. There's so many other ways that I can use my magic."

Dante presses a quick kiss to the tip of my nose.

"I'm so proud of you. The things you're accomplishing are astounding." He looks at me with wonder, and I feel my cheeks heat in response.

"And I'm proud of you. Not only are you this badass guardian, but you're my biggest supporter."

"Always." He tugs me closer until I'm practically half-sprawled across him. "That's better," he murmurs and presses a kiss to the crown of my head.

His heart thuds steadily underneath my ear. How do people survive losing their soul mate? It feels like every fiber of our beings is wound together into an intricate design. There's no clear distinction between us. There are no lines that can separate our souls.

I should probably call my dad later and check-in. It's been several days since I've heard from him. I can't wait until I can finally go see him. The program they have him in only allows phone calls at the moment. He has to be able to complete several steps before they'll grant him visitors. It seems like he's a prisoner, but I know it's for the best.

Emma

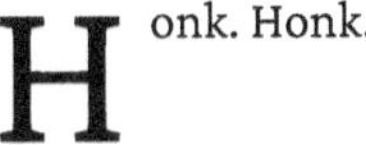onk. Honk.

I nearly jump out of my skin as I glare at the driver behind us. Ainsley and I are stopped at a four-way intersection as we try to figure out which way to go. All these roads look identical to one another.

"I'm moving!" Ainsley yells as if the person behind us can hear her with all our windows up.

"Pull over up ahead," I tell her.

There's a small gravel pull-off, and we careen into it, going full speed in Ainsley's little red car. We hit every pothole imaginable, and I swear we're one bump away from losing a damn tire.

"Are you trying to get us killed?" I ask, sweeping my hair out of my face.

"Sorry, I didn't realize it was that rough." Shifting the car into park, she searches our surroundings.

"Ya don't say?" I fire at her, laughing while I straighten my seatbelt.

"Let me see the map again."

I flatten out the thick paper and press down on the creases. The map got scrunched up as I saw my life flash before my eyes. The large rectangular road map shows all of Graystone, and I trace where I last knew we were with my nail. We should almost be there.

"Oh wait, you should've turned left at the stop sign."

"Ugh! I wish my damn GPS would work."

"What about on our phones?"

"Good luck getting any reception out here. This is considered the dead zone." Ainsley pulls her cell phone out of her pocket and shakes her head. "Nada."

Tugging my own out of my jeans, I roll my eyes. Of course not. That would be too easy.

"Okay, so we go back to the stop sign and go straight, then it'll be a right at the four corners. A left at Crossway Road and finally, "Not your average Witch" shop will be on the right in a light blue building." Ainsley runs her finger along the map as she speaks.

"Okay, straight, right, left, right. We got this. Punch it, girl."

Ainsley steps on the gas hard, and we kick up stones and dust in our wake. The music blares in the background, and I tap the beat on my thighs. I have to do something to get rid of the jitters. Before we know it, the little blue building with its dark windows comes into view. The coating on the glass is so dark that I can't even tell if there are lights on inside.

Ainsley brings the car to a more pleasant stop and turns to me. "You ready?"

Heck no. But she doesn't wait for my reply. As she opens her door, I scramble to unbuckle and follow her onto the small sidewalk. This shop seems like it's located in a ghost town. A truck and another car are parked down the road in front of what looks like a diner, but there's no soul in sight. This town brings out all the horror movie flicks I watched recently. I'm surprised there's not a tumbleweed blowing across the road.

My sneakers scuff on the rough wooden stairs leading to the door, and as we push it open, a squawking noise says, "Intruder. Intruder. Hit the deck!"

My head snaps to the side, and a fairly large African grey Parrot is perched on a branch with no cage surrounding it. I watch as the bird regards me like an actual guard dog would.

"Awe, who's a pretty bird?" Ainsley coos to the gorgeous but scary creature.

He walks closer to us, nearly to the end of his branch, and says, "I'll show you pretty bi-"

"Queen Athena!" An authoritative voice echoes through the room.

"Oooh." The bird squats lower, but I swear its beady eyes see through to my soul. "Intruder."

"I heard you, my little protector. Don't need to be nasty."

"Wasn't," Queen Athena squawks again, and I smirk.

"You weren't about to show them what a 'Pretty bird' does?"

"No!"

"I'm sorry you'll have to pardon Queen Athena; she's been moody lately." A woman with gray hair the color of the bird's feathers comes around the corner from a back hallway. "Do yourself a favor, don't say pretty bird in this shop; it triggers her attack mojo."

I'm pretty sure my eyes widen into saucers at this point. My heartbeat races while my breath shudders quickly from my lungs. Were we about to get mauled by a massive bird pecking out our eyeballs like a Thanksgiving feast? I don't think the words pretty bird will ever leave my lips again.

"She's a rescue, and unfortunately, she came from a rough household. They called her that, and you may not know it, but African greys are very intelligent birds with the capability to hold memories for a long time. So, as you may have certain words that trigger bad memories, so do they."

I didn't know that. I knew parrots were smart, but holding memories? "She is beautiful, though," I say as I take in her form, perched high on the bark and taking in our every move.

The woman's green eyes soften, and she shakes her head. "Poor thing hasn't always been that way. Most of her feathers were plucked when I stole her."

I gasp. "You stole her?"

"Damn right, I did. That and the other exotics those dummies didn't know how to care for." She hobbles our way with a cane.

It's hard to imagine this woman stealing anything from anybody. "I've always loved animals, and I actually wanted to be a vet. Do you have them all here?"

"I'm afraid not, sweetie. I sent them to live with other caretakers. I don't have the means to keep up with that many, but I couldn't part with Athena. She's an old soul like me." Her glassy gaze turns to the bird before returning those green eyes to us.

"What brings you two lovely girls in here anyway? Love potions?" She wiggles her eyebrows up and down, and I giggle.

"Actually, we were hoping to speak to Evie?" Ainsley asks.

"Evie, huh?"

"Yes." I nod. "Could you tell us where to find her?"

Her eyes narrow as she measures us up. "That depends on why you want to find her."

Ainsley looks at me. "Honestly, we just want to ask her how she helped half-breeds like us make it through the transition."

The wrinkles around her eyes relax as understanding sets in. Loud flapping from behind me makes me duck. Wind rustles my hair as Queen Athena zooms by and now rests on the old lady's shoulder. It bobs its head back and forth between us and the woman.

"This Evie. Evie intruders," it squawks.

The bird bobs her head again, and I let out a laugh. Ainsley joins in. This whole time, she's been right in front of our faces.

The old lady sighs dramatically. "Thanks, Queen Athena. What if they were here to hurt me?" She tosses her hands in the air.

The bird hunkers down and gets eye-level with me. Not blinking at all. My breathing intensifies as I prepare to run for my life. "Friends," she squawks loudly, making me flinch before my heart melts.

"You're lucky she likes you. I don't entertain guests anymore. But she's an excellent judge of character, so I'll make an exception for you two."

"Thank you, Miss Evie," I say and throw the bird a smile. "And you, Queen Athena. Parrots can have oranges, right?" I dig through my purse, knowing I still have some leftovers from breakfast.

"She can have a small amount, yes."

"Ah ha!" Finding what I'm looking for, I tear open the sealed container and offer a slice to the bird, who takes it gently and flies back to her perch by the door.

"Follow me," Evie instructs, taking us down the hall and into a room separated by a beaded curtain.

The scent of burning incense is heavy in the air, and the only light comes from flickering candles placed around the room.

"Take a seat."

Evie pulls out a chair opposite us and looks us both in the eyes for a minute before speaking again. My heart's in my throat. This is the moment we've been preparing for—the answers we've needed.

"Why do you want to transition?" She points to Ainsley first.

"I want to be an immortal. To prove to my father, who thinks so little of me because I'm only half his blood, that I'm worthy of him."

"Hmmm," she harrumphs. "You should only make the transition for yourself. How about you?" She stares intensely at me, and I get the strange feeling that she sees more than we think.

I swallow down the bile that's climbed up my throat. "I've always wanted to help people ever since I was little. Like I said earlier, I wanted to be a vet, but it turns out my father..." I take a deep breath and start again. "Is a bad man. He was using his doctorate skills to help an evil man cause atrocities that never should've happened. I want to be the doctor my father failed to become. I need to prove to everyone that I am more than the blood that runs in my veins. That his blood does not dictate who I am. That this is me, wanting to give my all to a cause I believe in."

"And..." she prompts. "What else, dear?"

Casting a glance at Ainsley, I feel guilty I haven't told her this yet. "My boyfriend said I'm his anima gemelli, and I feel it in my heart that he's different. Anima gemella different? I'm not sure, but I know a human lifetime isn't enough time to spend with him. I want eternity."

She nods in understanding, and I feel Ainsley's eyes burning holes in the side of my face. Regret sours my stomach. I haven't told Sierra yet either, and she's my best friend. I thought it was too good to be true as if I didn't deserve to have a soulmate after what my parents had done.

I cringe as I turn toward Ainsley. "I'm sorry I haven't told you that yet. This is the first time I've said it out loud."

Her hand grasps mine, and she smiles a wide-toothed grin. "It's okay. I'm happy for you!"

"Emma, I can help you with the ritual, but Ainsley, I'm afraid you're not ready yet."

We never told this lady our names. My awareness heightens. How the heck does she know who we are? Ainsley meets my eyes with the same question in her own.

"I'm not just a simple witch, my dear children; I am also a soul seer." Her emerald-hued eyes change to nearly gold. "I knew who you were the moment you walked into my shop. Which is why I can say with certainty that you are not ready yet." She cradles Ainsley's chin in her palm as tears glitter in Ainsley's eyes. "You will only be ready if you're doing this for you, not just to prove to your father that you are enough. If you can't see your worthiness without becoming something else, you will not make it through the transition. You need to find your own purpose in this world. Other than proving somebody wrong."

"How do I find my purpose?"

"In time, you'll be ready. The fates will show you when they believe you can withstand the change."

Chapter 11

Sierra

"**I** wish there was a way to clear this fog from my mind. I still don't remember him, Mom," I admit.

No memories have surfaced between being suspended from the academy and having my child. Raiden is down for his afternoon nap in his bedroom. He played a hard game of hide and seek today. The poor little guy was tuckered when I laid him down. His eyes fluttered closed before I covered him with his minky blue blanket.

"I hadn't wanted to mention it before because I'd hoped your mind would heal by now." My mom leans back against the kitchen chair. A strange look crosses her face as if her thoughts are somewhere far away.

Who am I to judge? I can barely keep my brain focused on the "world" I'm currently in. When I'm here with them, I think of Dante and the rest of my friends. When I'm back there with Dante and Emma, all I think of is my mom and Raiden. I drag my palms down the length of my thighs as nausea builds in my stomach. Not to mention, when I think of the prophecy, everything points to an unfinished job. I snap my attention back to my mom's watchful gaze.

"Mention what?" I ask, blowing across the mug of hot coffee in my hands.

She bites her lower lip as if debating whether to tell me or not. "It's a long shot, and I don't even know if it would help you."

"Just tell me, Mom."

She nods before tucking a stray wisp of brown hair behind her ear. "West Graystone has several caves hidden in the forest. One of them is called the Cave Of Anguish."

"Well, that sounds like a pleasant place to visit. Can we book a tour?" I roll my eyes. Who the heck comes up with these names?

A throaty laugh escapes her, and the grin reaches her eyes. Twisting her body toward mine, she puts her elbow on the table and rests her chin in her palm.

"It was originally named that because the stone it houses is rumored to be able to bring back the dead. Therefore, when immortals sought it out, they were filled with anguish."

Bring back the dead?

My head snaps up. Hope flutters in my chest like the wings of a butterfly. "There's a stone that can do that?"

"Among other things, yes. There's a large alexandrite tower tucked away deep within the cave. It's the most powerful gemstone in the world." Her words have me enthralled.

How come I've never heard of this before? Wouldn't they want that in a place where they can draw power from it? Questions flare to life in my brain like fireworks popping up in rapid fire.

"Then why is it hidden in a cave?" I ask.

"Our ancestors sealed the cave shut with a spell that'll only allow an elemental magic user through. That kind of magic could be catastrophic in the wrong hands. But with you, you could control the bad. You're strong enough to withstand it."

"I'm surprised with how power-hungry Excalibur is, he didn't get it already."

My mom's soft brown eyebrows squish together. "Why would he go after it?"

"Because he's evil and wants to control everything. He's actually the one that um..." I can't finish that sentence, so instead, I take a small sip of my miracle liquid.

The headache is beginning to form again. I've been getting them frequently for the past few weeks. No matter what I take, eat, or drink, nothing helps, not even sleep.

She takes a hefty gulp of coffee before responding. "Maybe he is in your fractured memories, but not here. In the real world, he's the lead enforcer of Graystone. He upholds all the laws and protects civilians. He's also not an elemental, so he wouldn't be able to gain access to it."

"He's not able to wield fire?"

She laughs. "No, but that would be an amazing asset to have in the field. Can you imagine the possibilities?" Her eyes widen, and a Cheshire grin lights up her face.

My stomach churns. I don't have to imagine; I remember every single detail vividly.

Huh. If Excalibur isn't an elemental and he's not the evil man my mind wants me to think he is, maybe I finally have lost all my marbles. I don't know; I still have a feeling he is. That kind of evil doesn't just poof away. That shit is soul deep.

This stone has me wondering. I set the still-hot mug down on the small table in front of me. "What else can this rock do?"

"As far as I know, there aren't any limits to what the tower can do. It's embedded with both dark and light magic within its color-changing facets." She smiles softly and looks off into the distance as if she can picture it.

"And why do you think it could help me?"

"Sweetheart, I love you, but I'm afraid you'll be stuck in this in-between state inside your head for the rest of your life. I want you to live a full and happy life." Mom reaches her hand to me and covers my own with her palm, giving it a gentle squeeze. "This could give you that."

"How do I know this side is real, though?" A war rages inside my brain, each side fighting for me to remember the truth. Each one holds the other captive while the truth fights to claw its way out. I think that's why I'm so exhausted all the time; my body is constantly in a mental war with itself.

She cocks her head to the side, and her face tightens. "Would I lie to you, sweetheart?"

"You have before," I state.

Her eyes narrow. "Every mother lies to her child at some point. That's how we protect you from things you aren't ready for. I wouldn't lie to you about something like this." She shrugs her shoulders. "What would I gain from that?"

That's the thing. In this version of my life, she wouldn't gain anything. My mom's just trying to help me like she always has. I'm just messed up in the head right now and feeling antsy and angry all the time.

"I know, I'm sorry." I sit back in my chair and sip my coffee while her words dance around inside my head.

A stone that could bring back the dead...

Ruby

I gesture for Liam, Waylon, and Bennett to go around the back of the building. It was reported to Nilo that a previous High Council member was staging a coup with a few other immortals. Our task is to put him and any others involved under arrest.

"We're in position," Liam's deep voice comes through the earpiece.

"Alright. Let's try to arrest them peacefully," I say before knocking on the door.

Movement from inside reaches my ears. I'll give him one more chance to come to the door.

Knocking again, I add, "Mr. Santiago, this is SIA Nine. I need you to open the door."

No answer. There's nothing but silence on the other side of the wooden door. Fine, we'll do this the hard way then. Swinging my leg up, I slam it against the door. It creaks but holds firm. I slam my foot against it again, and it breaks free, flinging wood chunks everywhere. The door bashes against the inside wall.

My team and I burst through the opening and begin clearing the rooms we walk by.

"He's here in the kitchen," River shouts.

Switching direction, I turn that way and halt in the doorway when I notice he has a gun pointed directly at the agent that found him. The muscles along my legs tense with the need to lunge at Santiago.

"Nobody needs to get hurt." I hold my hands up in the air. "You're under arrest for treason against the High Council. We're just here to execute the arrest."

He points the pistol at me instead. My agents trickle in behind me. There's a total of twelve of us on this mission. Three are still staged outside. This location was named the meet-up place for all the offenders, and I don't want to chance any of them getting away.

"I'm not going anywhere with you," he scoffs. "I should be the one in charge, not him. Instead, we were all removed from power so he can have it all for himself."

"You can take that up with the High Council. As you're well aware, we just follow orders. It's not our call to make."

River takes advantage of him being distracted by me and takes a step in his direction. Something clicks into place from the tile he steps on. The hairs on my forearms stand to attention, and my blood runs cold.

"Run," I barely get the word out when an explosion rocks the ground below us.

The blast sends debris flying everywhere. Taking a quick glance at the others, they have several cuts and what looks to be shrapnel wounds, but River?

Oh god, my stomach churns.

All that remains of him is scattered across the floor. His decapitated head rolls toward me, and I fight the urge to vomit. Snapping my head back up, I notice Santiago is no longer in the kitchen. His gun lays on the floor ten feet from where he stood.

My fists clench and unclench multiple times with the need to avenge River's death. My nostrils flare as I take in a shaky breath. My lungs feel as if they're on fire.

"Find him. Dead or alive, we're not leaving without him," I snarl. I'm not sure if I have the authority to make the call to execute a former councilman, but his treason charge has now risen to murder. If he were any other civilian, I could give that order.

I fight to hold in the sob that scratches its way up my aching throat. I need to stay strong for the others. They need a leader that can remain in control of the situation. My team draws their weapons and begins to spread out. Half of them search the house, and the others search the property. We came here hoping to take him without violence, but we were prepared for war. After all, he's trying to dethrone the current government.

Reaching down, I close River's eyes and promise him, "We will have justice for what he's done to you. Rest in peace, soldier; your duty's been fulfilled."

"Check-in," I voice through the comms.

One by one, my team states the all-clear. Where the hell did he vanish to? He didn't go by me, and there's no exit on the other side of the room. I kick at the floorboards and push at the cupboards, looking for a hidden exit. A piece of River's shredded clothing is pinched between 2 floorboards. Bingo. I shove my knife in the opening and pry it up. Sure enough, there's a cave below the structure, which wasn't on the blueprints we studied.

"He disappeared into a cave below the house. I'm going in. Look for exits." Leaving the doorway open, I jump down and land with a hard thud on the dirt.

The only light down here is filtering down from the kitchen above. Multiple sets of footprints weave a path away from the house, and the small lanterns on the wall aren't lit. I tug a flashlight out of my pocket and begin following the prints farther and farther from the house.

"Agents 1-5 come down into the cave; the rest scout an exit," I say quietly into the earpiece. If Santiago and his goons are down here, they probably heard me land anyway.

What sounds like a shoe scuffling up ahead alerts me to their presence just before something pierces into my shoulder, and I'm thrust against the dirt wall. A hand wraps around my throat in a vice-like grip.

I curse as the wound flares into pain. The flashlight falls to the ground but lights up several pairs of feet.

"Well, well, well, what do we have here?" The man holding me against the wall says.

His hot, raunchy breath fans my face. Damn, somebody get this man a breath mint. I try to pry his hands away from my neck, but it's no use. He doesn't budge. I still in his grip, trying to gauge the situation. Let them think they have me right where they want me. I'll bide my time waiting for the right moment to strike.

"This is Agent Nine; it seems the covert team is working together to bring us down."

Somebody strikes a match and lights a lantern. I suck a haggard breath in. I'm pretty sure it's an iron stake that tore through my skin and muscles. Rolling my shoulder causes intense pain, and I grunt. The bones don't seem to be affected. Hopefully, it's just the muscle.

"Not if they don't make it out of here," another man sneers. This one is balding on the top of his head, and his eyes hold a hard glint. I don't know his name, but I know I've seen that face before.

Shit, I need a plan. I can't take them all on my own, not in this shape anyway. Judging by what I saw in the flashlight beam and the little bits of light from the lantern, there were at least four of them—all men.

"There's far too many of them. I counted at least ten agents before we ducked below."

My team knows I'm here, and they should be on their way. Then, we can turn the tables against them. I have to keep them busy until then.

"Then we'll just take care of her. She's the one calling all the shots now," says the one with his disgusting hands on me.

"Screw you," I spit.

I wait until he inches closer to me, then I act. Smashing my head against his nose, he yelps, and I break out of his hold. I lunge for Santiago and slam my palms against his chest, shoving him against the makeshift wall. Fire burns through my skin with the movement. Holy crap, that hurt like hell.

"You've been trouble since the beginning. I knew you'd eventually turn on us," Santiago snarls in my face.

The others grab hold of me and pin me against the wall as I struggle to break free. It takes three of these weak assholes to keep me there this time.

"I'm following orders. Talk about calling the cauldron black. Aren't you staging a coup on the current High Council?"

"They shouldn't be in charge, and putting a witch on the council is blasphemy."

"And going against them is treason. This won't end with my team. They'll keep coming for you until justice is served," I pause. "And for killing River? I have a special kind of death planned for you asshole."

A soft noise filters down the hall, but the others don't seem to hear it. It's gotta be part of my team. I need to keep talking to cover up any footsteps that can echo down to us.

"So you're against the High Council now? What about when Ryker allowed Excalibur to run the show? Were you on board with that?"

"At least Ryker kept the old laws in place. There's a reason it hasn't changed."

"If you want to go by old laws, you should be executed on sight for treason."

"By whom, you?" Santiago puffs up his chest, and a dark chuckle comes out.

I flash a wicked grin. He doesn't know there are agents already swarming us. "You better hope it's not me."

His fist lands a blow to my cheek, and the coppery taste of blood fills my mouth. I swallow it down, not wanting to give him the satisfaction of spilling my blood. Instead, I smirk at him, daring him to try it again.

"You know why we named the SIAs by number?" He grins and leans his face closer to mine. "Because you're just a number. Nobody will miss you when you're gone. Your agent up there." He points to the dirt ceiling. "He'll be replaced by sundown. His death is just a number as well."

"That's where you're wrong," I say, my voice laced with venom.

I struggle against the hands holding me in place, and he backs away slightly. If I'm not mistaken, that's fear that flitted across his eyes. I force my body to be calm, and their hold relaxes just enough for me to bash my head into his nose next. Blood spurts out as he cries out in pain. I guess being hard-headed has its perks.

A twisted cackle escapes my throat before they smash my back against the wall. The force knocks the wind out of me.

Once I regain my voice, I tell them, "River had a wife and two kids. He has a country that will mourn his loss because, unlike you, the new High Council cares about their people instead of greed. We are not just a number anymore."

Something whizzes by me, and I freeze. A body drops beside me, and the men begin to shout and clamor over each other to get away. Now that they're not holding onto me, I grasp the stake and suck in a large gulp of air. On the exhale, I yank it out with a scream and fall to my knees. The stake skitters out of reach.

"You okay?" Jaxon asks while he steps in front of me to shield me.

"Just another lovely day in the field," I grit out.

"I got you if you need a minute. The others are chasing them down, and Liam found the escape hatch. They won't get away."

"Thanks, but there'll be time to heal after. I need to avenge River."

"Ruby... he was a councilman. Think about it first."

"I did. He's no longer a councilman, and he murdered an agent. If that were any-body else, we wouldn't have this conversation. Your concern is noted."

I snatch the iron stake from the ground, tuck it into my pocket, and stalk down the narrow corridor. Light filters through, and shouts ring out. Picking up my pace, I jog to the end. My wound screams in agony, but I push it down. Reaching a ladder, I climb up to find the other three men face down in the grass with cuffs around their wrists. My team circles them, waiting for orders.

"Well, well, well, now what do we have here?" I ask condescendingly.

I kick the one closest to me in the side, and he curses. Walking over to Santiago, I reach down with my good arm, grasp a handful of brown hair, and tug it back until he yelps.

"You killed an agent," I seethe, my vision only seeing red.

"Your point," he says before spitting in my face.

I wipe the nasty mix of saliva and mucous on my sleeve. This righteous son of a bitch. Tugging the bloody stake out of my back pocket, I smear it across his lips as he struggles.

"You taste that?" I don't wait for an answer. "I'll answer it for you. That's the taste of vengeance. You see, there's a new captain in town, and she doesn't take it lightly when somebody harms her agents just for doing their job."

I slide the sharp point down his chin and make swirly designs on his neck with my blood.

"You can't kill me. They'd never give your kind that amount of power." A slow smile spreads across his face.

"Wrong again." I smirk, pressing the sharp part into his skin just enough for the blood to bead on his throat. "Any means necessary to protect the people of Graystone. Your crimes are treason, murder, and assault on a defender of Graystone."

His breathing becomes rapid, and sweat rolls down from his hairline. My agents continue to stand silently around us.

"What do the laws say punishment for those crimes are?" I hedge and turn to my agents. "Any guesses?"

"That would be execution, Captain," Bennett answers cheerfully.

Santiago's face blanches. "No," he pleads. "You can't."

"So it would seem I do have that power. Let this be a warning to you two," I pause and look to my right, where the other captives are watching with wide eyes. "I will not tolerate any of my people being murdered. And I will not stand by while someone threatens the High Council."

I plunge the iron stake into Santiago's neck, and blood spurts out in an arc, coating my boots and the other two prisoners. He gargles and briefly fights to get free before his wounds prove fatal.

"You guys bring them to the Guard. I'm going to collect River."

"I'll stay and help," Waylon offers.

After the rest of my team disappears through a portal, Waylon and I walk back to our fallen soldier in silence. There's not much of him left. Tiny chunks of flesh and clothes are all over the kitchen. Taking a suitcase from the hall closet, I line the inside the best I can with sheets. I place his head inside, and Waylon grabs his boots and an arm. We lay his weapons beside him and say a prayer before lightly covering him with another sheet and zipping it up.

Waylon takes out his portal stone, and together, we carry River's remains to the morgue. Nilo's already there to greet us.

"Thank you both for serving Graystone. What happened today shouldn't have gone down. The team did well in bringing those to justice."

"Sir. I acted out of line," I begin.

"I know what happened. I've already been briefed on the situation. The correct punishment for his crimes was death. Though, next time, bring them here to face punishment."

"Yes, Sir."

"Now, for the worst part of our job." Nilo scrubs a hand roughly down his face. "We have to go tell River's family he won't be coming home."

CHAPTER 12

Eric

A knock sounds at my door, waking me from a fitful sleep. Groaning, I roll over and check the time on my cell phone, and it's nearly midnight. Who the hell would show up this late? Anger roils through me as I get up and stalk quietly to the door. I swipe the baseball bat from its place beside the tv stand on my way. I bet it's one of the little shits that keep spray painting my door.

Reaching for the handle, I whip it open with one hand while holding the bat in the other, ready to strike. They're not going to get away with it this time. I've had enough of this shit.

"Ah!" Ruby yells. "What the hell, Eric?"

Ruby stands on the other side of the threshold, wearing all her guardian gear. I toss the bat aside with a clang and step back so she can come through the doorway. Why would she come here this late? I haven't heard from her in days because she said she was working on a case.

"I'm sorry. I thought you were the painter." Relief fills me that it's her and not some shithead.

I'm too exhausted to fight anybody right now. The neighbors above me sound like they have a damn elephant running laps around their place at night. For the past week, I've been lucky to get five hours of sleep a night. My temper's been even shorter because of it. I snapped at one of the guys at work yesterday for nothing. Clicking the lock into place, I turn back toward her.

A strange look crosses her face. "The painter?" she questions, shifting her weight from one foot to the other.

"You know, the one that left me sweet notes on my door." I shrug as if that's a regular thing. Who knows? Maybe in this town, that's how they treat all the newcomers.

Ruby's shoulders relax, and she nods. "Oh, right."

She turns to look out the large window overlooking the town. A few lights are sprinkled here and there, but most people are sleeping at this hour. Something out there holds her attention, though.

"What other painter would it be?" I ask, drawing her gaze from the window.

"I don't know." She takes a slow, deep breath in. "Is this a bad time?"

There's a strange energy coming off her tonight. Her eyes look slightly puffy, and the dark makeup around them is smeared. From crying? I don't know what compelled her to come here, but I'd never turn her away. Wariness grips me in a chokehold.

"No. What's wrong?" I step toward her, needing to be closer.

"I had a tough assignment today." She unbuckles her weapons belt and sets it on the counter. "I lost one of my men."

Sorrow fills her eyes with a fresh coating of tears. I tug her into my chest, and she yelps.

"What's wrong?" I jump back and look her over. That's when I see the little bit of white poking out of her ripped shirt and the blood coating her clothes. "Oh my god, you're hurt?"

"I'm okay; it just hurts like hell when something touches it." She gives me a reassuring smile before wincing. "Or it moves."

Ruby slowly steps forward against my chest, and I gently wrap my arms around her, ensuring I steer clear of her shoulder. My chin rests on the crown of her head, and the familiar scent of her light flowery perfume drifts around me.

"I'm so sorry, Ruby." What else can I say? She probably can't even tell me what happened with all the clandestine rules this place has.

"I've lost other guardians while out in the field, but never one under my command. and not like that." She shudders against me.

"What happened?" I coax. I can only imagine what she's referring to. There's no limit to the creatures that go bump in the night.

We take a seat on the small couch in the living room. Her knee brushes up against mine, and to my surprise, she fills me in on everything that has transpired in the last few days. She didn't leave any twisted detail out. I'm coming to realize there's so much shady business that goes on behind closed doors. Their government isn't much different than mine back home in the States.

"Why don't you take a shower and stay here tonight?" I ask quietly. I need to know she's safe.

Her sad eyes flit to mine. "Are you sure?"

"Yeah, come on. I'll grab you some of my clothes," I say as I lead her toward my bathroom.

Turning the faucet on so it can heat up, I leave her to get undressed and into the shower while I search for something that would fit her. A pair of sweatpants and a rock band t-shirt it is. I knock gently on the bathroom door, letting her know before slipping my hand and the clothes through the opening and leaving them on the counter for her.

I pace the hall and living room, then back to the kitchen while I wait for her to come out. I knew her job was more dangerous than an ordinary guardian, but it didn't hit me until tonight. If her team hadn't gotten to her when they did, she could've died. What if she were the one to step on the bomb?

Running my hands through my hair, I tug on the ends, trying to ground myself. Her will to protect the citizens of Graystone astonishes me. How can she strap on those weapons every day and fight the monsters lurking in the darkness? How do any of them do it?

My mind spirals out of control until I hear her soft footsteps approaching me. Suddenly, I can breathe again. It's like she's the oxygen my lungs need to survive. Without her, they don't function as they should. Seeing her dressed in my clothes sends a pang through my chest. I've never wanted to be a better man more than I do at this moment. But with her, she sees all of me, not just the bad parts.

Her wet hair falls nearly to her eyes, and a haunted look crosses her face. Striding over to her, I brush the red strands off her face and kiss her forehead. We still haven't kissed since the day my apartment was vandalized, but the feel of her lips against mine is imprinted on my soul.

Ruby licks her lips before saying, "Eric, there's something I need to tell you."

I trace every inch of her face with my eyes. Tension pulls her skin into creases on her forehead and around her gorgeous chocolate eyes. I've never seen her look at me the way she is right now. Vulnerable and seeking comfort from me is a totally new level for us.

"You can tell me anything," I breathe. My heart thrashes wildly in my chest, and my stomach feels like it's grown wings.

"I want..." she hesitates, pulls her bottom lip between her teeth, and lets out a slow breath.

Far too many things can come after those two simple words. I don't want to get my hopes up, but she's here when she could be anywhere else in the world. She came to me at her weakest. I can give her the strength she needs. There's nothing she could want that I won't do my damnedest to give her.

"What do you want, Ruby?" I whisper. The beating of my heart feels like it'll smash right through my chest.

"You." Her palm lands on my chest, and a blast of electricity zips through me. I close my eyes and breathe in her words like a dying man. "I want you, Eric."

"Well, it's about damn time," I say with a grin spreading across my face.

Leaning my mouth down to slant over hers, I cradle her head in my hands and kiss her like she's the only sustenance I need in this world. Her fingers trail up my chest to wrap around my neck, and just like that, I'm a goner for this woman.

Ruby breaks the kiss to yawn, and I'm reminded of everything she went through today. Kissing her will have to wait until morning. And I plan to do plenty of that in the future.

"Let's get you some rest, okay?" I say breathlessly.

She nods, and another yawn escapes. Bending down, I lift Ruby and carry her to my bedroom, where the blankets are still messed up from my hasty wake-up. Gently lowering her to the mattress, I pull the covers back so she can get comfortable. I gently climb into bed on the opposite side and tuck myself against her. Ruby nuzzles her head against my chest, and her breathing slows.

I watch her sleep for what seems like hours before I'm able to fall asleep myself. Holding her like this while she's at her most vulnerable makes me feel like, for once, everything is the way it should be. Everything that's gone wrong in my life previously, I wouldn't change.

It all led me to her.

Excalibur

I've conserved my energy these last few days. The only dreamwalking I've done is with Sierra. I meticulously craft a dream world for my anima gemelli. She's been having a tough time adjusting to being locked up. She's taking it far harder than I imagined she would. My heart bleeds for her, and I can't wait to storm the Guard and set her free. In time, my love, that day will come.

Once everything about the dream is in place the way I want, I search for Rosalee. Finding her in the sea of dreams has never been an issue; there's an invisible tether joining our souls together. Latching onto it, I bring her to me.

A smile tilts her lips up, and she embraces me. Gods, I miss her. Her face looks gaunt. Her once full, voluptuous cheeks have hollowed, and dark circles frame her eyes. I need to give her hope that we're almost free.

"I think Sierra's ready to fetch the stone," I tell her.

"What is your obsession with this girl?" Rosalee snaps and throws her hands up in the air, releasing me and pacing the room. "Why can't we just be free and live our lives?"

Sighing, I take a step closer to her. I hate this, being stuck only seeing my mate in dreams where I can't even comfort her or save her from her own prison. The room we're in is our bedroom from our sprawling estate in Cancun. I've matched the neutral gray on the walls and the black satin bedding and drapes, even the wooden armoire that's behind her as she crosses her arms over her chest, effectively putting up that barrier she seems to like to erect when we don't see eye to eye.

"Because there needs to be a change in this world, and I'm the only one who can accomplish that." My nostrils flare, and the flames in the electric fireplace surge to life. "You've known this since the beginning. I haven't changed."

Her hazel eyes meet mine, and hold them steady. "But I have. I'm exhausted, Cal. I'm tired of always having to fight."

Her nickname for me cuts deep. She hardly ever uses it anymore. We've been together for just over a century and a half now, but I've watched the fight in her slowly wane. I knew this war was taking its toll on her and our relationship. I can't just turn off my duty to this world because she's tired of it.

"Soon, we won't have to, and we can ride off into the sunset if that's what you wish. But I have a duty to fulfill," I remind her.

Crossing the distance, I take Rosalee's chin in my hand and place a small kiss at the corner of her mouth to soften the blow. Wrapping her arms around me once again, she deepens the kiss before pulling away abruptly, and I'm left reeling. This woman is so hot and cold all the damn time it's frustrating. I try to keep my annoyance hidden from my face and tone of voice. She's irritable, and I don't want to waste the little time we get together fighting.

"Everything's going according to plan. The sleeping giants under the mountain are starting to wake," I tell her, hoping to improve her mood.

We're almost there. The dragons are my backup plan if Sierra doesn't succeed in stealing the alexandrite. The power lurking beneath those scales is enough to remove those who sought to imprison me. The dragons are my golden ticket to collecting the gemstones around each of their necks. They won't even see them coming; the dragons were on the island of Graystone long before those wards were in place.

Rosalee shakes her head and casts her eyes to the window. The ocean below is a beautiful bluish turquoise surrounded by white sand. We own half the island, and the number of humans that disappeared because they wandered too close usually keeps the locals away. However, I'm not above killing for sport; they make easy targets. Have a white sand beach, and these blubbering fools flock to it like sea lions during mating season.

"You can't control them." She shakes her head. "They're too powerful. Too blood-thirsty."

The flames ignite again and flare to life. "You underestimate my power, love."

She turns her attention to me and pegs me with a hard stare. "No. I see the threat that dragons will have on this world. I may not have been alive when they reigned, but I've seen what remains of civilizations who thought they, too, could wield and tame them."

"I don't want to tame them. They just have to do what I need them to do, and then they can return to the world they came from. I'll set them free." I take another step closer to try to close the gap between us.

"It won't be that easy." Her gorgeous eyes narrow, and a frown pulls her lips together. It's eery how similar Sierra's eyes are to her aunts, almost like a doppelgänger.

"I never said it would be easy," I say tersely. "If they want freedom in exchange for abiding me and breaking me out of here, then that's what I'll offer."

"And what if they don't want to leave after?" Rosalee sweeps her auburn hair off her shoulder, revealing the tip of the small flame tattoo surrounding a skull and crossbones just above her heart.

I have the identical one etched into my skin. It's the only physical link that proves we're connected, and it's not usually seen by others. She never wears shirts low enough to show that part of her skin.

I come to stand beside her in this room we've both loved and notice the tears glistening at the corners of her eyes. She tries to turn her face away, but I cradle her head in my hands. Inhaling her sweet perfume only makes me miss her more.

"Once this is all over, we can live here." I cast my glance around the room. "No more hiding, no more fighting. Just us, here, living the life we both want."

"You mean it?" Hope fills every inch of her face.

"I swear it on the oath I once made as a guardian. Once the order has been restored, I will lay down my sword and power and live happily beside you."

Rosalee tugs me in close, her heartbeat syncing with mine, and I relish the feeling of her in my arms once again. Even if she's not really here, we're both worlds away from each other.

But in this place, we're united once again.

Chapter 13

Sierra

Walking across the back lawn of the academy, I can't stop thinking about the Cave of Anguish. It's invaded nearly every waking thought. I've canvased every text or map trying to find it, and all I'm left with is a riddle that points to a place in the forest.

"Hello, Sierra," Yuri announces, yanking me from my thoughts as soon as I pass the threshold of the private training area.

"Hi, Professor Yuri."

"How do you feel about pushing your gift in a way you've never done before?"

"I'm always up for learning something new." Gift-wise, not school work, I add silently.

"I will show you my gift, but you must trust me." She has her arms clasped behind her back.

"Oookay." I draw out the word. I thought I trusted her, but this makes the hairs on the back of my neck stand on end.

"I'm a healer. There are very few of us, and we've all had to endure tough times in order for our gifts to emerge. Imagine the devastation that must be present for our bodies to earn the gift of healing." She waves her hands to her side, where a bottle of water and a small dagger sit on a wooden stand.

Dread builds in my stomach, and my arms sag at my sides. I don't like what I imagine that dagger will be used for.

"I'm going to show you how to channel your gift." She flicks a small fallen leaf off the knife.

"But I already do that?" I comment. "I can manifest icicle swords, bullets, lightning, and water bombs."

"Yes. But this is different." She reaches for the water and knife. "I need you to cut your palm and then take a sip of water."

My head lolls back; how did I know something like that was coming? "Really?"

"Trust me," she says, smiling as she hands me the dagger, hilt end.

Here goes nothing. I hold my hand up and away from my body and make a small, clean slice through the meaty part of my palm. A sharp pain ebbs as the blood bubbles up and drips to the ground.

"Now. Drink this."

I take a big gulp of water. And look at her expectantly.

"You see how nothing happened when you drank that?"

Well, thank you, Captain Obvious. "Yep."

"Give me the water bottle." She reaches out, clasps it with her hands, and closes her eyes. "I'm focusing all my energy on transforming this normal bottle of water into a healing potion. Each molecule is made up of three atoms. Two hydrogens, one oxygen. I'm picturing each atom and infusing them with my magic to become a drinkable healing potion."

Her breaths are slow and measured as she concentrates with her eyelids closed tightly together. The water begins to swirl inside the clear plastic and turn into a shimmery mixture of blue and purple with a little splash of orange.

"Take another drink," she instructs.

I do as asked and look to my palm, where the wound slowly starts to mend itself closed until it's just a soft white line. "That's so cool!" I exclaim.

Professor Zuri beams a radiant smile. "Now, don't take this wrong, but your gift is more destructive, so a weapon would be best to use."

I can't fault her for that. My gift is powerful and dangerous. I hold my hands out for her to remove the iron bracelets. Setting them on the table beside the dagger and water bottle, Zuri turns behind her and opens a large black case.

A long black and silver sword is pulled free from the foam it was nestled on.

"This is from my own personal collection, but I think it fits you and your abilities better."

"It's gorgeous."

"Tiny amethyst stones are embedded along the hilt to help enhance the user's channeling abilities. If you can master this weapon and channel your gift through it? You would be nearly unstoppable on the field." She holds the handle out for me to take.

It's lighter than I thought it'd be. As I twist it in the sunlight, the rays reflect and shine off the blade, which is a charcoal gray shade in the sun. The gemstones twinkle in the rays like fairy lights.

"Focus on the blade; imagine fusing your magic with the sharp edges of the steel."

Closing my eyes, I try to picture my magic flowing from my hands into the hilt and down to the sharpest parts of this beautiful specimen. Peeking an eye open, I notice nothing has changed, and I deflate a little inside.

"It's not working."

"Set it down, and let me see your hands."

"You're not going to cut me, are you?" I ask with an uncomfortable laugh.

"No," she answers with a chuckle.

She clasps both of my hands within hers, looks up to the cloudless sky above, and lets out a deep breath. A tingle formed in my hands when she touched me. Her eyes fly open.

"I can feel the burden you carry within you. There's trauma that's buried deep. Reiki may help you to heal your soul. Perhaps we'll add that into our training time?"

"Um. Sure?" What else am I supposed to say to that?

"Let's focus. You are one with the sword, child. It is merely an extension of you. You have to look at the weapon as a conduit of your gift. What will stem from it?"

Shrugging, I answer, "I don't know. A water gun?"

"Nonsense," she barks. The change in her tone surprises me. "You are the Immortal Savior, Sierra. The ancestors gifted you with magic that was not seen in a millennia. There must be a reason for it. The storm has not passed this quickly."

The prophecy comes to mind, and a strange feeling comes over me. "What aren't you telling me?"

"I've heard the whispers that war is coming. We must ensure you're ready to face whatever will come."

"Excalibur's locked away where nobody can get to him." I hear the doubt trapped within the syllables as I say those words. Something in a distant memory wiggles in my brain like a sliver, like a little thorn wedged into my skin.

"Evil like him spreads like a disease. There's always going to be somebody who will take the mantle and continue to bring wrath to the Earth. Our world is changing rapidly, and the only thing we can do is morph ourselves into the righteous protectors of Graystone. Take that anger and fear and make it your most lethal weapon. Channel all that pain into your magic and down into this sword."

I grasp the hilt with shaky hands as her words' ramifications trail over my body like spiders. I knew it wasn't over; deep down, I've always known that. Clenching my jaw, I hold the sword pointed up to the afterlife where my mother and all the rest of our friends who died on that battlefield rest. As I focus all of my power into the metal within my palms, a sob rips out of my throat as the last of my energy is expended. A bright flash lights up the darkest corners of the woods as the sword begins to glow.

The colors flow in jagged bolts like lightning, ranging in colors from white, pink, purple, and blue. My breathing is haggard with the effort to keep the magic contained. It wants to fly, to expel at a target.

"Now!" She shouts, and immortal guardians immediately surround me from all sides. They must've been lurking in the forest. At my confusion, she yells over the wind that's begun to whip around us, "Fight them, Sierra. Fight as if your life depends on it!"

"I don't want to hurt them! I don't know what it can do!" I cry out desperately. Looking face to face with all the guardians standing before me, some seem familiar, but I don't recognize them. There must be about twenty forming a large circle around me.

A groan escapes me as I struggle to contain the magic. My arms tremble. I don't know how long I can hold it back.

"These are some of our best fighters, and if you do harm them, I will heal them." Zuri claps loudly, "This is the only way to know how to use your power. Now strike!"

Three guardians come at me all at once. After a brief hesitation, I swing the sword to stop another blade from hitting me. Lightning cracks from the tip, striking a nearby tree. The guardian's eyes widen, but that's the only visible sign he shows as he continues to push against mine. Another guardian advances behind me, and I squat down, then jump up and spin my blade in a circle around me, connecting with hers, and a gust of wind blows her back. My ponytail swings in the wind as it circles me. Light licks up the sword's edge, almost like little flames dancing in the turbulent air.

I continue fighting, but it's obvious they, like Dante, aren't giving their all against me. It's one thing to spar with them, but using my gift against them doesn't feel right. I'm starting to think Professor Zuri is a certifiable nut job. I don't know how to take my power back from the sword without expelling it at somebody.

They take turns striking and blocking; all the while, lightning flies from the blade, and they narrowly miss being struck. Rain trickles down into a steady stream, soaking the ground below us. I try to reign in the magic, to pull it back from the sword, but it's almost like it has a mind of its own.

"Stop dancing in the rain and bring the storm!" Zuri cries out.

"I am!" I shout above all the noise.

"Not hard enough!" Zuri reprimands.

Zuri wants a storm. Fine, then. I twirl the blade above my head and slam it down with all my might into the Earth below my feet. Thunder booms above us in a deafening roar, and the ground splits apart as lightning travels through the water and tosses all the guardians up in the air, only to land about thirty feet away with a thud that silences the storm raging around us.

Shit!

"Oh my god, what have I done?" I gasp and cover my mouth. The sword's light diminishes back to looking like it had previously.

Releasing my grip on the sword, it falls to the ground, and I race to the nearest guardian but see he's moving to get up. I hold a hand down to help him, and he takes it with a grin. "Good job, kid." He brushes the dirt off his pants.

"Are you okay?" I search across his form to try to see any noticeable wounds. But I don't see any.

"Never better," he answers.

Turning to look behind me, I notice they're all getting up, looking completely unscathed. Some have minor cuts and bruises, but they fade before my eyes.

"How?" I ask, turning my attention to the professor.

"I gave them all a healing elixir before you arrived, and their armor is specially formulated to withstand lightning, among many other things. I knew you couldn't hurt them too badly."

"You knew it would spawn lightning?" I accuse. "What if I killed them?"

"They knew the risk, and we took precautions. As for the lightning," Yuri pauses to shrug. "I wasn't one hundred percent certain, but after our training we've had, that seems to be the most prevalent for destruction."

Feeling utterly drained, I sit down on the grass. I yawn and stretch my arms above my head. My muscles tighten before finally relaxing. Digging into the cooler Professor Yuri brought, I snag an elixir and a granola bar.

"How do you feel?" she asks me.

Another yawn. "Drained," I reply. "And a little scared, to be honest."

"Scared of yourself or your magic?"

I ponder that thought and find myself thinking about the first and only battle I've been in. Many of Excalibur's followers weren't there of their own will. He controlled their mind.

"Both. I've seen immortals be manipulated, no longer in control of their bodies. What if that happens to me? I could be the ultimate weapon primed to fight against my family and friends."

"If you live your life worried about others manipulating you, you'll never know peace." She brushes her feet across the weeds to flatten them before sitting beside me. "You're destined for greatness, Sierra; you'll be able to handle more than other immortals can withstand. I would think if he could use compulsion on you, he would've done that in India. Maybe you have an extra layer of protection in your mind?"

True. If Excalibur wanted to, he could've. Rosalee could get into my head only long enough to instill fear, but I pushed her out.

"Maybe."

If that's true, then maybe I can wield the alexandrite tower, bring back the fallen, and keep the darkness away. I could shield myself from the dark magic's effects. I can feel the power calling to me, and I think this is what I was meant to do. It's not too late to save them.

"You are the storm, Sierra. Never forget that. Next time we start practice with you being the storm, not ending it that way."

I am the storm.

Emma

I awake with a jolt, bolting upright and gasping for breath—another nightmare. I glare at the dream catchers hanging above my bed. Even though it's pitch black in my room, and I know it doesn't feel things, I want it to know I'm not happy. The dream catchers were a welcome gift from the academy; every student received one. With feathers and gemstones, each one is in matching shades of crimson. They said it's to keep our minds fresh for learning.

I scoff. I wish I could send it back; it hasn't done a good job of keeping bad dreams away. I don't remember many dreams, but I hear Sierra scream or make other noises far too frequently for them to be useful. That or I didn't realize how sinister her night terrors were.

My heart rate begins to slow as I take several long, deep breaths. This nightmare hit far too close to home. It was about Eric getting cornered by some of the immortals who don't want us here. He hasn't told me if he's had any more graffiti on our apartment door.

Snatching my phone off the nightstand, I rub the sleep from my eyes. Ugh, six o'clock. My first class doesn't start until eight; I could've slept for another hour. Not wanting to disturb Sierra, I decide to stay in the warmth of my bed. Unfortunately, once I'm awake, I can't fall back asleep.

In an effort to keep my cell phone's light from waking Sierra, I turn my body toward her bed and begin playing a mindless sorting game on it to pass the time. My mind drifts to Maverick. I haven't told him I'm going to do the transition yet. I'm waiting for the right time to drop that bombshell on him. I know it won't go over well, but Evie has assured me we have plenty of time to make me ready.

A while later, the sounds of alarm clocks and doors shutting reach me through the thin walls of the dorm. Putting my phone down, I glance at Sierra's bed and find she's not even in it. I get out of bed, walk across the room, and flick the light on. The only thing on her bed is a laundry basket that was there when I went to bed last night. It's not unusual for Sierra to return to our dorm after I'm fast asleep or leave before I wake up. She's been doing a lot of extra training sessions with some of the professors here.

The part that is unlike her is that she didn't return at all.

The laundry basket is in the exact same spot as before. We always tell each other if we're staying elsewhere. With all the crazy stuff that's been thrown at us, we can never be too careful. I go through my texts to see if I missed something. But, no, there's no message. Dialing her number brings me straight to her voicemail.

An uneasy feeling settles in my stomach. Something's not right. I check Sierra's desk and nightstand for a note or anything to give me a clue as to where she is. She didn't leave anything for me. Grabbing a set of clothes from my bureau, I dress quickly before trying her cell phone again—still nothing.

Feeling that uneasiness snake up my spine, I plop down on her bed. Her journal lands on the floor with a soft thud. A blue and purple galaxy stares back at me, baiting me. Sierra began writing in that book several weeks ago when she said she started having strange dreams.

I promised her I wouldn't read it. She'd tell me when she was ready. After all, I still haven't told her about Maverick being my anima gemella. Guilt creeps in and twists my stomach into knots. I should've told her by now.

Snaking a hair tie of hers, I sweep my long blonde hair up in a messy bun while I debate on breaking my promise. Would Sierra understand? After everything she's done for me, I owe her. If Sierra's in trouble, I need to help her.

I gently pick up the journal from the floor and sit back on Sierra's bed. My fingertips trace the words on the cover, and I squeeze my eyes shut.

"Please don't be mad," I whisper into the empty room.

Resolving myself to break that vow, I begin flipping through quickly. This proves that there's a lot written here. I settle for a random page in the middle.

"Hazel eyes, brown hair, maybe 2?" Her scribbled handwriting reads.

I scrunch my brows, trying to figure out what that means, before reading the following line.

"Dante's cabin. Pancakes. Kitchen."

Still no help. I wipe my sweaty hands on my jeans before turning to another page with only one word. But it takes up the whole page. The letters are repeatedly scratched into the paper with several lines of blue ink.

"MOM?"

"What the heck?" I mumble before diving in even further. Some of the writing is hard to understand as if she were rushing to get it all out.

Is she still having dreams about Sophia's death? I know for a while after the battle, she suffered from flashbacks. I can't imagine the agony of watching your parent die over and over again.

I begin flipping the pages faster and faster, skimming over everything as my mind grows darker. She mentions a place called Cave of Anguish and how it's been calling to her. Her mom told her she could use it and stave off the effects of dark magic. That Sierra's strong enough to fight it.

Even from my research into the transition, I know not to mess with dark magic. So, what's been calling to her?

The next page reads, *"I found it."*

Oh my god. What if I'm too late?

CHAPTER 14

Dante

"Dante, I can't find Sierra," Emma cries into the phone.

"What are you talking about?" I press the cell phone closer to my ear.

"I-I don't think she returned to the dorm last night." Emma gasps.

I run a hand through my hair and fist the back of it. I was out late last night raiding a compound of rebel werewolves, and I didn't call her when I got back because it was past three in the morning. I squint at the green lights of the clock on my nightstand—seven thirty in the morning. Putting the call on speaker and tossing it on the mattress beside me, I throw on a pair of clothes.

"Tell me everything," I demand.

"I think it would be best if you see for yourself. I went through Sierra's journal, and it's fucking dark, Dante," she whimpers. "I don't know how I missed this."

I'm too tired to decipher what that could mean. Grasping my blue benitoite portal stone in my palm, I direct the beam to the center of my room. "I'll be right there."

The portal swirls around and around until I can see the dorm room Sierra and Emma share on the other side. Stepping through, I clap my hands together and close the doorway, pocketing my stone. Emma's dressed in a light blue long-sleeve shirt and dark denim jeans. Her long blonde hair is pulled up high in a messy bun on the top of her head. Her usually bright blue eyes are weary and puffy from crying. I hold my hand out for the small notebook she's clutching to her chest.

"Nothing's been touched since I went to bed last night." Emma gestures to the side of the room, where a perfectly made bed and a basket of clothes sit atop it. Her lower lip quivers slightly. "I promised her I wouldn't read it."

"Yeah, that was before she pulled this. Hand it over." I swallow thickly as Emma places the worn-edged notebook with a galaxy cover in my outstretched hand.

Once I open this, I'm invading her privacy, and there's no going back. I try again to reach out to her with our shared bond. Vaguely, I can feel her. My hand wraps around the emerald amulet that rests just above my heart. I close my eyes and take a deep breath, searching harder for that link. The spell that links the necklaces together thrums in my veins. It's close, much closer than the woman herself. Gritting my teeth, I yank open the top drawer of her dresser with a screech, and her matching amulet stares up at me from her folded clothing. Her cell phone sits beside it.

"Son of a bitch!" I shout.

Emma gasps behind me once her eyes land on the gemstone. "Why would she take it off?"

"Because she doesn't want to be found," I growl, slamming the drawer shut with enough force to rock the bureau against the wall. What the hell is she up to?

Sitting on Sierra's bed, I begin to flip through the pages. The front pages are more bullet points of random things. The blood that's been boiling just under the surface turns colder and colder until it's nearly ice as I read about the confusing dreams she's been having. The following sentence makes everything blur together.

My mom said the alexandrite tower could bring back the dead. I think she's reaching out to me from the afterlife and guiding me on how to help her and how I can make up for all the pain I've caused. I could bring them all back.

I pinch the bridge of my nose and squeeze my lids tight. I know the stone she's referring to. I came across it while researching Excalibur before Sierra's transition. All I know about it is that the ancestors hid it behind a potent spell to keep anybody from getting to it. The dark magic fueled with the light magic inside the alexandrite could overpower any other witch or warlock's spell. The tomb can only be accessed by a... oh no.

Only somebody gifted with the elements can get through the spell protecting its whereabouts.

Tightness forms in my chest, choking me and making my breathing hard. Please let it not be what I'm thinking. I flip to the last page.

I can feel the tower the more I research it. I know it exists. I can fix this. I will fix this. Please forgive me if I fail.

This is what Teiresias's warning meant. I know it clear as day. This was the darkest vision he was referring to. You can't mess with dark magic without paying a heavy toll.

Shit, baby. What have you done?

My fingers fly over the keys of my cell phone in a group message asking them to meet me at my log cabin. I portal Emma and myself back home before others trickle in. While I wait, I make photocopies of her journal entries. The more eyes on this, the better. We need to find the location of that stone before it's too late. I fill them in on everything I know once they all arrive.

"The cave's in West Graystone. I don't know the exact location, but it's deep in the forest," Nilo speaks up for the first time.

"What are the chances it really could be Sophia?" Emma asks quietly.

"Zero. Sophia would never want Sierra to harness black magic, even if she could bring them back to life. Sophia sacrificed herself for all of us; don't tarnish her name like that," Joe snaps at Emma, and she winces, taking a step back as if he struck her.

Maverick jumps up from the table, and his chair crashes backward with a smack. "Watch what you say to her. It was just a damn question."

At the same time, Eric jumps up and says, "What the fuck, Joe?"

Joe rubs his temples hard. "Sorry, kiddo."

The pieces start stringing together in my head until they paint a very disturbing puzzle.

"I bet everything I have, Excalibur's doing this. He's using my gift of dreamwalking to reach her. The dreams about her mom and our son are all his handiwork." My stomach plummets. Pointing a finger at Nilo, I growl, "I told you they needed more protection. You assured me she was safe, and there was no way your *brother* could get to her."

All eyes swing toward Nilo, the brother of our enemy. Suspicion filters across their gazes as they take in his rigid posture. All this time, I thought he was working with us; maybe he was always working against us, and we'd just been too blind to see it.

"You better walk that thought right back, Dante," Nilo's voice hardens. "I had nothing to do with this. He's bound by wards and surrounded by iron. How the hell was I supposed to know he could do that?"

"You know more than anybody what he's capable of. Why would he want Sierra to have the alexandrite?" I question.

Nilo's brown eyes widen before he scrubs his large hands over his face and inhales deeply. "Because she could use it to set him free. That stone would be able to over-power our containment spell," he says quietly.

"You've gotta be kidding me," Ruby grits out as she throws her head back and lets out a frustrated yell.

"We have to find Sierra before she gets to that cave. If she harnesses dark magic-" Maverick starts.

"I know." I slam my fist down on the wooden table. The unfinished edges are rough, but the top is smooth with a coat of shellac. Which now has cracks spreading out from where I hit it.

Dark magic isn't something somebody can just dabble in. It changes them for the worse. There's always going to be something that pulls them to use again, like an addict. One hit is never enough; it'll just keep luring her until she gives in. Each time dark magic is used, it blackens the soul. There's no going back. There's no soul scrubber to clean off all the grime, no magical bleach to take it all away. The darkness that's already within her will bloom like Teiresias predicted could happen.

Fuck!

"We made copies of her diary. I'll hand each of you different pages. If she found it, so can we," Emma instructs them.

I skim over my pages to find anything that hints at the location. The cavern in my chest splits open the more I read. Sierra was spiraling, and I wasn't around enough for her. It's all right here in black and white. I've been too busy with my job to care for her as I should have. It may have cost me everything.

Cost the world everything.

"I think I found something," Reid says, grinning. "*The Cave Of Anguish is said to be hidden behind a waterfall, and the entrance blocked by a thicket of sweet briar rose.*"

Finally, some good news. "I used to hike in the mountains. I think I know where the waterfall could be. Grab whatever you need to go hiking from home. We move out in five minutes. She already has a head start on us, and I'm not wasting any more time."

"Agreed," Joe says.

"We'll find her in time." Maverick rests his palm on my shoulder before guiding Emma into a portal.

I nod to my best friend. God, I hope he's right. I stalk into the bedroom I share with Sierra. My eyes land on the bed. I can't go there. She's coming back home. Yanking a black hoodie off the hanger and slipping it over my head, I string my weapons across me. I walk back into the dining room and read through some more pages while I await the others. My finger traces a discolored spot on the paper where it looks like a tear slipped down and smeared the black ink.

"I'm coming for you, baby."

Sierra

I swat the millionth mosquito away from my face that's tried to eat me since I came into the forest. Crunch. My ankle twists painfully after slipping on a moss-covered stone. I let out a pained growl. Crap, that hurts. I've been walking for hours and still haven't seen or heard that damn waterfall yet. Sliding down to the ground, I swing my legs in front of me in a stretch while I suck in a slow deep breath and place my palms on the ground.

"Come on, water, where are you?"

There are too many water sources nearby to be able to pinpoint a waterfall. Like a heartbeat in my veins, I can feel the droplets sitting daintily on the ferns beside me, the liquid deep in the Earth below me, and the moisture hanging thick like mist in the air. I thought it was going to be easier to find than this. I should've known better. It's hidden for a reason.

I tug the map out of the small bag and unroll the faded, yellowing parchment. I was right where the waterfall was supposed to be when I arrived, according to this ancient map—the northwestern mountain range just past the volcano. The volcano's smoke billows up into the sky, meaning it's still active. It may not be erupting at the moment, but it could anytime.

I'm running out of daylight, and the forest isn't a good place to traipse around in the dark. I search the ground around me for something sharp, and my fingers graze over a dark rock with a pointy end. It'll have to work. Next, I pull the small vanilla candle out and scrape some leaves out of the way so it can be even on the large boulder next to me.

Sucking in a deep breath, I set the clear quartz pendulum on the map and light the candle with a match. Taking the sharp stone I found, I slice it into my palm and let a few droplets of blood fall on the map below. I pick up the long chain of the pendulum and swing it in a small circle over the entire map.

"Ancestors, I call on thee. Guide me to the place I seek. For the power that resides inside will allow the past and present to collide." A powerful gust of wind circles around me and pushes the pendulum to spin hard in circles until it's almost parallel to the map. "My will is strong, my morals defined, bring me to the alexandrite tower, and I will be aligned. I offer the blood of the Immortal Savior as payment for a favor. I ask this of thee. So mote it be!" I shout into the densely wooded area.

The quartz continues to circle round and round as the droplets of blood combine into one. Ever so slowly, the blood trails across the map toward the mountain with the waterfall in front of it. That's where I am already. The trail continues to carve a path until it reaches the back side of the mountain and stops. I wait with bated breath to see if the blood will move again. The pendulum slows of its own volition until it ultimately stops moving altogether.

The blood stalls behind the mountain, not in front of it! I've been searching all this time where the map depicted the water, but it couldn't show the back of the large mass. I blow out the candle and dump the wet wax on the rock that held it steady. The drips of blood lift away from the map like steam on a hot mug until there's no residue left on the map, as if nothing happened at all.

After packing all my supplies back into my bag, I roll my ankle back and forth, making pain shoot up into my calf. I'll have to take it even slower now. Just great. But at least I know where I'm headed. A bird chirps out a song above me. Looking up into the dense canopy of leaves and limbs, I spot the little songbird, a Chaffinch. They're all over Graystone. The round underbelly is an orangey brown with a slate gray color wrapping around the back of their head. They were a frequent visitor to Dante's cabin.

Dante. My chest aches as I think of him. I hope he can forgive me for this. In time, he'll understand; I know he will.

I push the air out of my lungs forcefully. I miss him so much. The last time I saw him was this past weekend. I know it's only a matter of time before Emma realizes I haven't come back and calls him. Then the cavalry of friends will be called in to try to find me like the last time I took off on him after my mom's and several others' funerals. I just need time. I took every precaution I could so he couldn't track me.

Dante wouldn't be on board with what I'm doing. I'm not stupid. I researched everything and know there's dark magic in the alexandrite. Dark magic taints the heart, or so it says.

But what if my heart is already stained? What if I can't continue this life without trying to right my wrongs? I'm the Immortal Savior for a reason, and I'm strong enough to withstand the darkness that'll call to me once I use it the first time.

If my mom thinks I can do it, I can. Everything happens for a reason. I was put on this Earth to save people, and that's what I will do. Pushing myself back up to stand, I gingerly step on my hurt ankle. Muttering curse words under my breath each time I put weight on it seems to help. If only just for a second.

Pausing at a fork in the woods where the walking trails veer off, I try to remember which way I went at the last junction. I think I went right. I've already gotten turned around in the dense thicket of trees more than once. I've never been a forest type of girl. Never learning to navigate them prior to this venture may prove to be my downfall.

I won't give up. I will find the waterfall. I will cut through the pink rose briars to get to the cave that holds captive the stone I need. I wish I could have brought my music with me. I focus better when I have a beat going in my head. I'll have to make my own. I start singing along to one of my favorite songs. It's awfully convenient, but it's about losing my way.

I lost my way a long time ago, but I'm on the right path now—the path of redemption. Zuri's premonition floats through my mind about me needing to be the strongest

I can be. I don't think I can be strong enough without my mother. But I can be strong enough to keep us all safe once she's back in this world where she belongs.

Chapter 15

Dante

My boots sink heavily into the decaying leaves and small twigs. Inhaling the deep, earthy scent of a remote wilderness eases some of the tension between my shoulders, but not much. We're close now. Sierra has to be around here somewhere. I narrowed down about a ten-mile block of land where I believe the waterfall her notes are referring to is. I've only seen that body of water once and thought it was strange it wasn't on the map. I guess I know why now. They didn't want anybody to find it.

A screeching noise greets me as Emma freezes beside me. The eerie call stops and the forest is left in silence after. Not even a cricket dares to chirp.

"What is that?" Emma asks, stepping closer to Maverick's side.

"Most likely a hawk. We must've spooked it," Maverick answers while he tucks an arm around her lower back.

"That didn't sound like any bird I've ever heard." She shudders.

We quickly check the devices in our ears to ensure they're working correctly before we split off into two-person groups. I'm antsy, and my nerves are shot. I need to find Sierra. I reach out with our bond again, trying to feel her presence, but only a vague awareness reflects back at me. Not enough to tell me she's close.

I should've taken a step back from being a guardian. I was warned this could happen and didn't put her first. I'd sign my resignation letter now if it meant I could go back and ensure she was okay.

Joe strides through the brush to come up beside me. "I'll be the eyes from above."

Without waiting for an answer, a cloud of smoke envelopes his body, and he emerges as a large bald eagle. The flap of his strong wings pulses the air around us as he takes off above the canopy of leaves.

We've been walking for miles without finding any evidence of Sierra or the cave.

"I found the falls," Eric's low voice cuts through the silence.

A tiny bit of relief floods me as I finally fill my lungs with a large gulp of air. "Where are you?"

"We're about forty yards northeast of you, Dante," Ruby instructs.

I yank the folded map out of my back pocket and spread it wide. Tracing the blue lines that circle the location they were scouring, I place my finger in a rough estimate of where they should be and tell them, "Got it. I'm on my way."

"We'll be right there," Maverick insists.

I portal to them quickly. "Call out."

"Here."

Jogging toward Ruby's voice, other voices chime in to find them. The sound of water rushing begins to get louder the farther I walk. My heart slams in my chest, wondering if we're too late. Deja vu hits me when I step into the clearing. The small pond sits in a low canyon. Above the ridge, this place is lined by towering trees. Joe wouldn't have been able to spot it from the sky. Water flows freely from a drop of about thirty feet. A small deer drinks from the pond on the other side. Her ears twitch as she decides if we're a threat.

Not willing to wait for the rest to catch up. I bolt toward the waterfall on the narrow path that leads behind it. Small droplets mist my face as I careen to a stop just on the backside of the water. The inlet to the cave is blocked by gnarly-looking rose bushes.

The pale pink blooms that cover the branches are about the size of apples. Searching every inch of twigs and stems, I find no opening.

Either Sierra hasn't found the location yet, or she found another way in. How can something this beautiful hold something as horrible as that tower?

Tugging at the branches to gauge how stuck they are, red hot pain lances through my palm. "Shit." I yank my hand away as a blister forms. That must be where only an elemental user can get through.

"It's the cave, but I don't think she's found it yet. We should stage ourselves around the area and wait to ambush her. Nobody approaches her but me, got it?"

Mumbled yes's reach my ears, and I lean against the stone away from the thorny vines.

We wait for what seems like hours, with only the sounds of the forest to drown out the silence. What if Sierra already got through it?

"She's coming up on your right," Maverick whispers.

I swallow. "Okay, stay where you are."

I don't know how she's going to react when she finds out we're here to stop her. I'm praying Sierra's not being mind-controlled by Excalibur and that we can reason with her. I tilt my head to the side, and a strong pang hits me in the chest and surges through my veins as I watch her limp on her right foot. She's hurt. That's probably why she couldn't find it sooner. I hold my breath as she sidesteps behind the trail of water.

Oblivious to me, her focus remains on the dark thicket of rose briers speckled with pink roses. She carefully pushes her hands into the center and begins parting them. Her arms reach farther into the briers than mine were able to.

"Stop."

Sierra flinches and yanks her hands back. As she turns, the branches snag on her arm, leaving angry scratches in their wake. Her beautiful hazel eyes fly wide open. "What are you doing here?"

Reaching a hand out to hers, I answer, "I can't let you do this."

"I know what I'm doing, Dante," she snaps and pulls her hand free.

"Do you, though? Do you know what that kind of magic will do to you?" I soften my voice, trying to reason with her.

"I can handle it." She limps in front of me to the barrier.

"No, you can't. That's why it's hidden away from everybody. Power like that isn't meant for anybody to wield. It's too powerful."

"I'm not just anybody. I'm the Immortal Savior. I can bring them back."

"Okay, let's say it's true that you can fight the darkness that's trying to consume you. Do you know what happens to those brought back from the afterlife?"

She leans against the smooth stone beside the roses, taking the weight off her bad foot. "I don't have time for this."

"Why? What's the rush?"

Her shoulders sag. "I know you're not going to change your mind, and you won't be able to sway mine either."

"Answer the question," I command in a hard tone.

"I know about the side effects, damn it. I'll find a way that doesn't happen."

My nostrils flare. She's stubborn, but I don't know how much brainwashing he did to her. "Their soul will be broken. Forever split between the living and the afterlife. There's no miracle cure for that. No magic spell that heals a shattered soul. There's nothing you can do to fix it. The peace they found up there." I point my finger to the sky. "Will be stolen from them, and they won't be able to return. Can you really do that? Can you be okay with sentencing them with a half-life full of misery?"

She blinks and shrinks back as if I've wounded her. Her eyes search mine for a beat before they harden. "I'll never be your equal, will I? You'll always think you know better. You don't trust me."

"Sierra, you are my anima gemelli. My queen. I'll never be your equal because you are so much more than I could ever be. You're more than I could ever possibly deserve, yet you're mine. Fate tied us together for a reason, my love. I do trust you, but Excalibur weaseled his way into your mind. He planted this information there, not your mom."

Hurt flashes across her face, and she winces. Sierra shakes her head. "No. It's her. I can feel it."

I grasp her arms and tug her into me until she's against my chest. Cherry blossoms invade my senses. I sigh as I rub a hand down her back. "As much as I want to believe that, and I know you do, too. Sophia would never want you to use dark magic. She'd know the cost to you would be too great."

"Our son was there too," she whispers. "He needs us."

My throat closes up. I saw in her journal that our little boy was with her in that dream realm and that he was the same boy from the visions Teiresias showed her. She never talked about those visions with me. She locked them all away like she had the rest of her pain as if she could keep it all buried. But nothing ever stays buried.

"I'm not sure how Excalibur was able to pull it off, but I'm telling you, it's not real. Sophia knew her destiny and the part she had to play in the prophecy."

"What if she found a loophole?"

"There's no loophole with our destinies. A while back, Teiresias helped me to learn about mine. Do you want to know what that is?"

She nods against my chin—her skin goosebumps under my palms.

"To be the light in the darkness for the Immortal Savior. It's my destiny to ensure you continue to see the light and not succumb to the darkness."

Sierra rakes in a sob as her fingers twist in my hoodie. "I'm sorry, Dante."

"I'm sorry for not being there as I should've been. I don't care what you say; I'm quitting." She tenses in my arms. "I'm putting you first. Let the other guardians step up and deal with the chaos the dark ones create. I need to take care of you." I place a kiss on her forehead. "We'll get through this together, just like I promised."

Another sob tears out of her throat. "I'm so sorry, Dante, but I need to do this for them. I love you."

A strange sensation washes over me, almost like something's tugging at my skin. Sierra cries harder, her whole body trembling as her breathing becomes rapid. My head feels dizzy, and I try to suck in a breath, but my lungs won't expand. I gasp for air as she steps out of my embrace, tears trailing down her cheeks. Her hands are fisted at her sides. She won't even look at me.

That's when I know.

She wasn't saying she was sorry for what she did. It was for what she was about to do. My vision clouds as the realization sets in that she's using her gift on me. I don't think she could bring herself to kill me, but she's still under Excalibur's spell. I slowly reach one hand up to her as I drop to my knees. My other hand wraps around my throat, willing it to allow air to pass through. How can she do this to me? Pain lances through my heart, a white-hot, searing pain that forms within our bond. Can she feel it, too? The crack she's putting in us?

"I'll bring Lucas back, too. I'll get them all back. I promise everything will be okay." She swallows thickly. The sound of my friend's name on her quivering lips cracks my heart open even more.

"Sierra, please stop," I choke out. How can she hurt me like this? The thought of causing her any harm absolutely repulses me. I'd die before I harmed her.

My thoughts begin to turn fuzzy. The pulsing of blood in my veins slows to a crawl as if my blood is the consistency of syrup. Time stands still as I watch the love of my life drain me before my eyes. She bends down to kiss me on the forehead before turning on her heel to leave me here. I muster the little bit of energy I have left to snatch the iron handcuffs from my back pocket and slap them on her wrist before collapsing on my side.

My body wracks with a coughing fit as I heave fresh oxygen into me. Sierra shrieks and draws my attention as Maverick tackles her to the ground on the narrow walkway. Her face hits the stone with a painful smack, and I wince. Maverick locks his gaze with mine for a moment before the others filter in around us.

"I'll never forgive you for this!" Sierra screams out, thrashing her body against the cold stone below her.

"Yeah, well. Some things aren't easily forgivable," I snap, pushing the words through my scratchy throat.

Stalking to the waterfall's edge and disappearing on the other side, I have to put some distance between us. I can't even look at Sierra after that.

"Dante, please," she cries out from behind me. "It's my fault they're all dead."

Still not regaining my equilibrium, I lean back against the rough bark of a tree, sliding down and scrubbing my calloused palms across my face. Is this what it feels like to have your life destroyed?

"What if they got it wrong? What if she's not really my anima gemelli? Is everything I feel for her just an elaborate lie?" I whisper as I feel that crack in my chest turn cavernous.

"Did she really do what I think she did?" Maverick's voice breaks me out of my own twisted thoughts. His dark eyebrows dip down.

I clear my throat as I stand up. "Yeah."

"Shit, man. What are you gonna do?"

The ache lodged in the center of my chest begs me to forgive her. Deep down, I know Excalibur messed with her mind, but I don't know what this means for us. I feel her presence before she steps out from behind the wall of water, with Nilo leading her with a hand on her forearm. Now that she can't use her abilities, she can't block our bond. Even without the necklace tying us together, an overwhelming amount of sadness and bone-deep grief envelopes me. When her watery gaze lands on mine, she sucks in a ragged breath as guilt washes over her.

I clutch at the ache in my chest, which nearly makes me fall to the ground. The hurt of what she did echoes all around us. There's no going back after this. What she did is unacceptable. Everything in me tells me to wrap my arms around her and hold her tight, that everything will indeed be okay. But I can't. I don't want to be anywhere near her.

For the first time in my life, I want to be as far away from my mate as possible.

"Dante, I-"

"Don't," I cut her off and hold a hand up. "Nilo, is there a safe place you can take her where he won't be able to reach into her mind?"

"While she's awake, yes, but while she's sleeping, I'm afraid that'll be in your wheelhouse." He frowns.

"I haven't been able to dreamwalk with her in months." I pinch the bridge of my nose, still refusing to look at Sierra. I wonder if I couldn't reach her because he was there already.

"I may have a solution for that. If I can shield Sierra's mind with my ability, I think I can keep him out long enough for you to get in," Nilo offers.

After all these months, I longed to spend more time with her. Now that I have the option, I don't want to. It's what I have to do, though. Even with me mad as hell at her, I'll still protect her any way I can. That's not something that can be stolen as easily as the water in my body.

"Let me know when everything's all set. I'll be at my cabin." Reaching a hand into my pocket, I rub the smooth sides of my wand-shaped portal stone. It's never felt so cold to me before today. I never thought I'd be using it to get away from Sierra. Pointing it at the ground, a large oval forms and swirls away the forest.

"Wait," Sierra whispers.

"I can't talk to you right now, Sierra."

Once the portal is fully formed, I step through and don't look back. I trust my team to keep her safe. Any of them will be able to do everything I can. When the time comes for her to sleep, I'll be there. But until then? I need space to breathe and work through what the hell just happened and what it means for us.

Sierra

Watching Dante walk away from me hurt more than I ever thought was possible. It felt like he ripped the air right out of my lungs and took it with him. I still feel like I can't breathe. My lungs are stuck in the same position, slowly losing more and more air. But that's what I deserve. I never should've used my gift on him.

I could've found another way or waited him out. Instead, I'm left with the image of him falling to his knees, gasping for breath with agony in his eyes. The cave had a fitting name, but only they had the reason wrong. The anguish wasn't about the dead; it was about shattering the person who means the most to you in this horrible, messed-up world.

"What if they got it wrong? What if she's not really my anima gemelli? Is everything I feel for her just an elaborate lie?" His heartbroken questions keep replaying in my mind until a silent sob tears its way out of my chest.

Besides the stray glance in my direction, the rest of our friends barely look at me. I'm unsure if they know what I did to Dante. Maverick does, though. Every time his stern gaze sweeps over me, his eyes narrow. Nilo is standing to my right, and Ruby's on my left. I don't know if they think I'm a threat. Since Dante encased my wrists with these iron handcuffs, they've left them on me as if I'm a damn prisoner, just like back at the academy. At least there's no chain linking them together.

"Are you okay?" Emma's voice drags my face to look back up from the ground.

"No, I'm not." I try to swallow around the lump sitting in my throat. I'm not okay and haven't been in a very long time. I just mastered the art of hiding behind a mask to make everybody else feel better.

"What can I do?" Her thin, light brown eyebrows squish together.

"Let me out of these." I lift my hands up to chest level. "So I can get to that alexandrite and bring everybody back that died because of me."

"That's not happening," Nilo says, glaring at Emma. The warning is clear on his face, not even to attempt to help me.

Her pale blue eyes soften, and her lips turn down. "It's not your fault they're gone. I thought we'd already been over it. I thought you were past this?"

"How can I ever get past this? Especially now that I know there's a way to make up for it." I twist my aquamarine ring around my finger, begging the wetness building in my eyes to dissipate. "I can bring Mom back," I whisper.

"It doesn't work that way. Once the soul has left this plane, it can't be reunited completely with the body. It's a fate worse than death if you bring any of them back," Nilo says quietly, and his eyes take on a faraway look.

"Then why would my mom tell me about it?" I question.

"Because it wasn't your mom that was telling you. It was Excalibur." Ruby places her hand on my shoulder, trying to soften the sting of her words. Ruby's shoulders snap upright, and she grasps my left arm. "Nilo?"

My gaze drifts down to my arm. The veins on the inside of my wrist are black. The dark lines start at a now-closed wound at the base of my palm. The dried blood on my skin must have been from when the rose bush dug into my skin when I yanked my arms back.

"The briers must've been imbued with dark magic." Frowning, he twists my arm to look at the other side. "You've been marked by the Goety. Each time you attempt to use black magic, the darkness will grow until it reaches your heart."

"And then what?" I ask quietly, my gaze enraptured by the trails inking from the base of my hand. He doesn't answer for so long that I raise my head to look at him. His lips are in a tight line, and wrinkles form around his eyes.

"If you're consumed by dark magic, there is no cure." He swallows and rakes in a deep breath. "You'd find yourself in a prison a lot like Excalibur's."

My eyes flick back down to my wrist. My throat's suddenly dry, and my blood pulses loudly in my ears.

A few hours later, locked away in the Caribbean castle, my mind is my worst enemy. Replaying everything that happened and the things I wasn't able to do. And the worst of it is what I did to Dante. I'll never forgive myself for that.

"I just want to see her one last time." They won't let me go to bed until Dante's here. I'm exhausted. I didn't sleep at all last night, and I haven't seen or heard from Dante since he walked away this morning. They've told me he's coming to guard my mind while I sleep. That way, Excalibur can't reach me.

"But it's not her," Maverick barks.

I have a hard time believing it's not Mom. Everything about her seems the same. I don't see how Excalibur would know all her little traits or how she'd pat my hand when she's worried about me.

"Even if it's not, I want to say goodbye. Can't you give me that, at least?"

Maverick stares at me for a moment without speaking. My heart thuds against my breastbone while I wait for him to decide. He sighs deeply. "Fine. But if Dante gets pissed at me, that's on you."

"Thank you, Maverick."

"While you're in there, ask Sophia something only she would know the answer to." His eyes have an icy sharpness to them I've never seen him deploy.

I already planned on it. The need to prove them all wrong burns hot in my veins. "I will. Good night."

"Good night, Sierra."

As I'm walking to my bedroom, Maverick's footsteps sound behind me. Irritated, I whip my door open, quickly step inside, and try to close the door, but his hand blocks it from shutting.

"I'm sorry I can't let you out of my sight." He turns his face away from the opening.

What? "Are you serious?"

"Orders are orders." He half-shrugs with the arm, not holding the door open.

"So Dante's okay with me getting changed in front of you? How about showering, huh? Are you gonna stand in the stall with me? Will you soap up my luffa, too?" I practically spit the words at him.

"Don't make this harder than it has to be. Obviously, I'd turn around while you do those things." A rosy hue tinges his high cheekbones, but his eyes still hold a coldness.

"This is unbelievable." Have I lost all of my freedoms because of this?

His eyes widen as he snaps, "No. Do you want to know what's unbelievable? What you did to Dante. If you'd do that to him, there's no telling what you could do to the rest of us." His jaw locks tight, and his breathing quickens. His tall frame towers over me as he looms this close. Maverick's nostrils flare in and out with every breath.

"I can't even use my magic," I spit out between clenched teeth, stalking away from him. The cuffs around my wrists need a key to unlock them.

"We're not taking any chances. That stone you tried to get to is capable of helping Excalibur escape. Did you know that? That one tower can undo the spell that holds him. That would mean all those lives were lost for nothing. Your mother died for nothing."

My breath hitches. No, I didn't know that. The wheels spin in my mind over and over again. Could that have been Excalibur's plan all along? To trick me into getting the alexandrite tower for him? I wouldn't put it past him. He is a manipulative son of a bitch.

"I didn't know," I answer honestly.

Maverick crosses his arms across his chest and leans against the wall just inside my bedroom. "Well, now that you know, is the stone still as alluring?"

I shake my head.

"Go to sleep. Say goodbye. Move on." He continues to glower at me from the other side of the room.

"You say it like it's easy," I bite out.

I yank my bureau drawer open and swipe a tank top with a matching set of shorts. My thumb rubs along the soft material. The dark purple garments are Dante's favorite, and he's told me they make my eyes stand out even more. Turning to face Maverick, I wave a finger around in a circle for him to turn, and he does.

After what seems like ages, I'm finally able to fall asleep. I awake in the dream realm in the bedroom of the log cabin Dante, and I share back in Graystone. Taking a deep breath, I toss the covers back and clamor out of bed, slipping my toes into my plush slippers at the foot of the bed. I hesitate with my fingers resting on the silver door handle. I've never wanted to be right so much in my life as I am at this moment. She has to be real.

Creeping down the hall, the sounds of a kid's TV show reach my ears. It's not just my mom I'm saying goodbye to. I won't see Raiden again, either. Well, at least not until he's born. But where do I stand with Dante? I'm unsure if that future's even a possibility now.

Raiden's sitting in his little highchair, shoving a fistful of cereal in his mouth.

"Easy there, Ray. That's a lot of Cheerios." I rub his back.

He beams at me. "Mama want O's?" he asks, sliding his plastic blue bowl toward me.

"Sure, buddy. How can I say no to this handsome little face?" I lean down and kiss his cheek. The scent of baby shampoo lingers on his skin. I wrap him in a tight hug. I don't know how much time I have before Dante busts through my dreams, and I need answers. I choke down a few pieces to make him happy. I can't eat knowing what could happen.

Sizzling draws my attention to where my mother stands in front of the stove, frying bacon and eggs. She turns just before I reach her and embraces me. My arms pull her in tighter, and I try to memorize every last detail. The floral perfume that swarms around me, the soft brown strands of hair that press against my face, her strong arms holding me as I fall apart on the inside. But most of all, her voice as she says good morning to me.

"I love you and miss you so much," I tell her.

"I love you too, sweetheart, but I'm right here. There's no need to miss me." Her fingers brush my hair back from my face.

"It's not the same, though." Now that I know it could all be a sham. I'm looking for anything that could be a clue to what the truth is.

"Everything's going to be okay. Once you get that alexandrite tower and heal your mind, you'll see." She smiles at me.

Steeling myself with a deep breath, I step out of her hug. "Do you remember that gaudy bright orange bike I got for Easter when I was five?"

I never had an orange bike in my life. I've always hated that color. Mine have always been purple, pink, or other girly designs. And I was terrified of riding it for years, so it sat in our garage collecting dust until I was way older.

"How could I forget?" She grins. "You loved that thing. We had to practically pry your hands off from it when it was time to go into the house."

My stomach plummets. I was wrong. This whole time it hasn't been my mother I've been spending time with. It's been *him*.

"Didn't even need the training wheels." I force out, still wanting to be right. I had training wheels up until I was ten.

"Never, you couldn't wait for Dad to take them off." She flashes another toothy smile before using a fork to turn the bacon over.

I feel nauseous. Bile stings the back of my throat. I was wrong. I was so very, very wrong.

Nodding, I turn away and find my son still cramming cereal into his never-ending pit of a stomach. I hug him harder this time as he squirms and tries to pull away. I'm not ready to say goodbye. A lone tear slips out, trails down my face, and splashes onto his tray. It's that moment when I realize how much love my mother had for me and what she was willing to sacrifice for me. A mother's love is a powerful force.

There's nothing that could rival the strength that now beats like a drum in my veins.

I have to let him go now in order to have a chance at having him in my life later. But how do you say goodbye to your son whom you've only just met but love more than anything in this world? I'd never felt anything close to it before. I thought the battle with Excalibur and losing my mom would be the hardest thing I'd have to endure, but I never imagined this. How could I have predicted this scenario?

What will losing Raiden do to me if I'm not already broken beyond repair? Another tear spills out and drops beside his bowl. The small drop flattens but stays still as if frozen in time.

My chest heaves in a strangled breath, and it feels like that fireball Excalibur had once put in my stomach is now lodged firmly between my ribs and my heart. Slowly engulfing the organ in flames until nothing remains but a pile of ash that could be carried away in the wind. This is what a shattering heart feels like. A pain that is truly grown from despair.

A pain that could end me if I allow it to.

But I won't give it that power. Excalibur has no idea what he just did. The fury he unleashed inside of me.

"Mama loves you so much, Raiden. I'd move heaven and hell and fight Satan himself to keep you safe." I force myself to swallow the acid rising in my throat. The burning slowly grows more and more intense. My voice wavers with the effort of keeping it at bay. "I will fight for you, your dad, and our future. I'll never stop, Ray." Taking in another shaky breath, I whisper, "I'll never stop."

"Wuv you, mama." His small, chubby cheeks rise into a smile, and it's as if he can see through my thoughts. Ray's little hazel eyes widen as I lean down to place a final kiss on his forehead.

His sweet little voice is still echoing in my mind as the dream is ripped out from beneath my feet, and I'm back in my bedroom clutching a pillow to my chest. The ache of losing my mother yet again fills my body, but losing my son, regardless of being real yet? Nearly shatters me to pieces.

The pain from that loss is bone-deep. Each pulse of my heart is like another fracture in my soul, chipping it off piece by piece. I cry out in agony and curl up in a ball, feeling a pain that's far worse than what I endured during my transition.

Chapter 16

Dante

Sierra whimpers again in her sleep. I can't believe Maverick let her fall asleep without me here. I know she wanted to say goodbye to her mom, but it's unsafe. Reid's currently in Italy sourcing ingredients for a spell that will help keep Excalibur out of her mind. At first, I wanted to wake her immediately, but I decided to play it out and see how it went. It's not like he can do more damage than he's already done. I'm sitting on the chair beside the bed, watching her sleep. So far, she's mumbled a few things about a bike and tossed and turned in the sheets.

I lean forward, my elbows on my knees, and rest my head in my hands. A headache pulses hard between my temples. The crack I felt in the bond earlier today is still there like a sliver inching its way deeper and deeper.

How could she hurt me like that? How can I continue loving her with everything inside me and knowing she could easily do that? Does she not feel the same level of the bond as I do?

"Mama loves you so much, Raiden. I'd move heaven and hell and fight Satan himself to keep you safe."

Hearing her talk to our child hits me like a freight train I never saw coming. After I left her this morning, I read the rest of her journal. Every single pained word until the words blurred together from the ink smearing from her tears as she wrote them. She's sad and confused. Initially, Sierra didn't remember much from the dreams she shared with Excalibur, but the more he came to her, the more she'd recall when she awoke.

She wrote about Raiden a lot and said she doesn't understand how I could have been gone away working so much and missing all the milestones he's reaching. That hurt. If we had a family, they'd be my first priority. I wouldn't be missing everything. But that's my fault she'd think that, since I didn't see how bad it was for her. I offered to cut back on work, but she told me not to. I shouldn't have listened.

The worst part of it all is that she one hundred percent believed Sophia could reach her from the afterlife. Once she can finally see the truth, it'll crush her. I know it will. She's never fully processed the grief of losing her mother.

Sierra squishes the pillow harder to her chest as tears trail down over the bridge of her nose and wet the pillowcase. "I will fight for you, your dad, and our future. I'll never stop, Ray," she whispers before her face contorts as if in pain. "I'll never stop."

Her sobs grow louder, almost more than I can take.

The way she's saying the words is as if she knows the dream world she's spent so much time in lately is fake now. She's said her goodbyes to both of them. Sitting on the edge of our bed, I gently nudge her shoulder. "Sierra, wake up," I rasp, my voice hoarse.

Her eyelids flutter open as she blinks a few times. Looking down at the pillow in her arms, she closes her eyes, sobbing harder and curling in on herself. Coaxing the pillow from her grasp, I lie down beside her and pull her onto my chest. Rubbing her back as her salty tears soak my shirt, I'm at a loss for what to do.

I'm still hurt over what she did to me and trying really hard to put myself in her shoes, but in every scenario, I'd never hurt her the way she did me. But I'd be lying if I said I didn't want to take all the pain from her. That I didn't want to be the one to fix everything for her, make everything right again.

"They're gone," she cries out. Her voice is so full of heartbreak that it steals the air out of the room.

"I know." Tightening my hold on her, I nearly crush her small body against my chest.

"I never should've used my gift on you. I'm so sorry, Dante." Her hands fists my shirt, clinging to me as if I'm all that holds her here.

Weighing my words, I decide just to be blunt. "You're right. You shouldn't have."

Her voice wavers as she says, "I don't want you to leave me."

I squeeze my eyes tight, wishing I could take back what I said this morning. I didn't mean to say them out loud. "I'm not going anywhere."

"But you said-"

"I never should've said that." I kiss the crown of her head. "Us? We're not a mistake. Destiny doesn't make mistakes. I was angry and hurt that you did that. I don't understand why you didn't come to me when you started having these dreams. I could've helped you."

"I didn't tell anybody. It wasn't fair that my mom could reach out to me, but you couldn't see Lucas." She buries her face into my side.

I tilt her chin up with my hand until she's looking into my eyes. "I'm glad you got to say goodbye to her, even if it wasn't really her. Not many people get that kind of closure. And I don't care if something's fair or not." I rub my thumb over the soft skin on her chin. "If you're happy, I'm happy. You're sad, I'm sad. You're hurt? Everything in me would shred to pieces to make you whole again. *You* are my world, Sierra."

Her watery gaze holds mine. "You're everything to me."

Leaning up, I place a featherlight kiss across her lips. "Will you tell me about him?"

"Who?" Her red-rimmed eyes search my face.

A smile tugs at the corner of my mouth as I tell her, "Our son."

She smiles back as her eyes gloss over again. She places her palm over my heart, and I clasp my hand over hers.

"He's amazing. He looks just like you but has my eyes. He loves blueberry pancakes and playing hide and go seek." She laughs softly. "Oh, and blowing raspberries on his belly makes him giggle uncontrollably. Anytime he hears music, he feels it deep inside and has to dance or bounce to the beat. I wish you could've met him."

There's a sadness in her eyes, a longing for that little boy. It pulls at me like nothing I've ever experienced before. With everything inside of me, I want to give her that. I need to give her the son she dreamed of, but not yet.

"I will when the time is right for us to start a family." I'm not ready to begin that venture just yet.

"And when will that be?" she asks, hope filling her features.

"Well, with the chaos surrounding us right now with the dark ones, it's unsafe for anyone. Besides, I want to enjoy you all to myself for a while." I grin down at her. There's no rush for me to have kids. We'll have plenty of time for that later. I want to know everything there is to know about this beautiful, multi-faceted woman next to me.

"Even though I love Raiden for a name, and it's fitting because it means thunder and lightning, if there's a chance Excalibur chose it, I don't want to name him that."

I nod my understanding. "I heard you tell him that you'll never stop fighting for us." Her sharp intake of breath tells me she thought I couldn't hear. "How about Helios? After the Greek god of the sun." I caress the side of her face with my knuckles. "He can be the light that keeps you anchored." Bringing her wrist, stained with dark magic, to my lips, I press a kiss there. "Together, he and I can keep the darkness away from you."

I don't quite understand how dark magic latches onto somebody or how to get it out, but Willow's coming tomorrow morning to help us. Whatever comes our way, we'll handle it together as we should.

"Helios Ray Xavier." Her smile is radiant and contagious. "I love it."

She snuggles in closer until no amount of space separates us. We lay like that for hours, her sound asleep in my arms and me watching over her mind to keep intruders out. Soft rain falls outside and splashes against the window, playing a soothing lullaby for me. I have to fight to resist. In the distance, a low rumble of thunder breaks up the cadence of the shower.

My cell phone's emergency warning system blares in the quiet room. Snatching the device off the nightstand, I swipe at my eyes and reread the message on the screen.

"What is it?" Sierra asks groggily, stretching her arms over her head.

"Mt. Glenshaw just erupted."

"Hasn't it done it before though?"

This volcano resides on the northwestern side of Graystone, conveniently in the same mountain range we were in yesterday. Coincidence? I think not. If this had happened yesterday, we could've been burnt to a crisp in the lava.

"Yes, but not like this. It blew the whole cap off the mountain, and lava shot up over twenty thousand feet in the sky. The ash cloud that'll form from that can be catastrophic."

"What do we do?" Sierra looks frantically around the room.

"We're safe here in the Caribbean."

"What about home?"

"I don't know," I answer honestly, racking my brain to remember my past history classes. It's erupted like this before, long before our time.

"I can help stop the ash cloud from covering Graystone," she pauses, "With my gift."

"After everything you just went through-"

"These are our people, our home." She rises from the bed and tugs the bureau drawer open. "We have to help."

Eric

A shrill alarm rouses me from a deep sleep. Reaching for my phone, my apartment rocks like an earthquake. The cell phone crashes to the floor with a slap while the alarm continues to blare through the speakers.

Finally holding onto the device, I swipe my finger to light up the screen and freeze.

"Volcano?" I question into the otherwise dark and quiet room.

I read the same words repeatedly, thinking I'm wrong. I didn't even know there were volcanoes here. Rushing to the window as I tug my jeans on, I peer out. The streets are still shrouded in the early morning darkness, and I can't see anything in the sky. Lights start flicking on one by one in the surrounding buildings. Others must be awakening to the same alarm.

Snatching my portal stone from the side table, I slide it into my pocket and dial Emma while throwing a t-shirt on.

She answers on the first ring, "Eric?"

"Are you okay?" I ask, not concerned that I may have woken her up.

"Yeah. I'm at the castle. You?"

Oh, thank god. I don't know how close the eruption is to me, but I don't want Emma anywhere near danger. It seems that no matter how hard I tried to keep her away from this immortal world, she finds herself stuck right in the middle of it. A shout reaches me through the thin panes of glass.

"Stay there," I demand. "I'm in Graystone, and the volcano just erupted."

"I heard. Come here with us; it's safe here," Emma pleads.

Panic seizes my chest when I realize I don't know where Ruby is. She better not be anywhere near where that thing blasted open the Earth. She can't always tell me her assignments, and I understand, but it doesn't lessen the worry.

"I need to call Ruby," I rush out.

"She's still here, Eric." Emma's yawn comes through the device.

We separated after Sierra went back to the compound safely. I wasn't needed there and didn't want to feel like a third wheel. We haven't told anyone we're together yet.

It's all still new, and I don't want to do anything that can jeopardize our relationship. The glass of water rattles on my nightstand as another powerful aftershock shakes the city. More panicked cries come from outside.

"You're sure?" I question, grabbing the glass and dumping its contents in the sink before it can crash to the floor.

"I'm pretty sure. Ruby went to bed just before us." A rustling noise comes through the line as if she's dressing. "We're on our way down to the dining room, and I'll let you know if she isn't."

Yesterday was such a disaster. What Sierra could've mistakenly let out of that cave makes a shiver run up my spine. I've always known dark magic was a horrible thing to mess with, but for it to have its teeth into Sierra is appalling. Sierra's grasp on her powerful gift has been rushed and unsteady. That power being used by dark magic? That's a world I never want to see.

We hang up and I look out the window to try to see anything outside, but the night sky still holds firm. I can't see a damn thing except for the lights of the town and people running outside. Clamoring down the stairs and pushing the door open, I'm met with smoky air that smells like rotten eggs. Immortals and witches talk loudly, and I can only catch bits and pieces of their conversations.

"Dark forces are near!" an older woman with graying hair and coke bottle glasses yells as she scurries into another building.

Somebody rushes past me and bumps my shoulder. It wasn't hard enough to hurt, and everything's in turmoil down here at the moment. I let the action slip off me. There's no need to make a crappy situation worse.

"Father!" a small child cries out. Snapping my head toward her, I watch as her dad heaves her up into his arms and sprints across the street.

Twisting on my heels, I see a group of enforcers surrounding Nilo, the master council. A few other enforcers are standing watch several yards away. Was it a targeted attack?

"Where's the volcano?" I ask the first man I come to.

He blinks and looks like he's debating on running the other way, but instead tells me, "On the northwestern side. In the forest."

My stomach plummets. That's where we were yesterday. The cave that held the alexandrite tower Sierra sought is on that side. I have a hard time believing that's just a coincidence. Maybe she did unleash something, but we didn't even realize it.

My phone chimes in my pocket with a message.

"Ruby's here," says Emma's text.

Another message comes through, this time from Ruby. "Are you okay?"

Some tension releases knowing my girl is safe. Ignoring the chaos ensuing all around me, I create a portal to the castle in the Caribbean. I'm thankful that it's far from Graystone. The effects of an eruption shouldn't be felt there. I imagine the rest of the citizens will also be leaving Graystone until it's safe to come back. But if the citizens aren't protected by the magical wards that surround Graystone, can they still be protected from the dark ones?

As soon as I close the portal and pocket the benitoite, Ruby rushes to me on the front lawn.

"Are you hurt?" She pats me down.

Warmth spreads through my entire body at her concern. I wrap my arms around her and suck in her familiar scent while nuzzling her neck.

"I'm okay, I promise."

I can't describe the feeling of having her in my arms and knowing she's safe. Any free time we had the past couple of weeks has been spent together. Emma stands just in front of the large door to the castle, smiling as she takes us in. She throws a wink my way before turning on her heel and dashing inside. Welp, cat's out of the bag now.

Sierra and Dante rush outside and disappear through a portal. Worry sets its claws into me. She should be resting, but no doubt they're off trying to save the world.

CHAPTER 17

Sierra

Colors swirl together like a cloud of smoke, faster and faster until the haze dissipates and the outskirts of the forest come through. We step through, and the soft moss absorbs our footsteps.

Smoke floats in the air around us, and the smell of sulfur burns my nostrils. The dawn of the sun is just barely peeking above the horizon, but the rays of sunlight are muted.

I have no idea how to actually stop the mushroom cloud of ash billowing high above us. But I have to try; I can't help but feel the eruption is tied to me using dark magic yesterday.

I hold my hands out for Dante to unlock the cuffs I'm still wearing. The brief hesitation in his eyes cuts deep. Wariness flashes in his gorgeous green eyes, but I turn to look at the ground. My cheeks burn, and tears fill my eyes. I did this to us. I'm the one who built that mountain between us.

Dante grasps my hands one a time and releases the iron from around my wrists. I rub at the tender red marks that wrap around where my arm meets my palm. The metal bit into my skin, but I was too embarrassed to ask them to loosen them.

Bringing my hands up in front of me, I act like I'm squishing a ball. The ashen cloud's edges tighten, but not nearly enough. This will probably take more energy than I have.

"Call Reid and Konstantina. I'll need their strength. And we need to get higher." Turning around in a circle, I notice there's a peak of a mountain just high enough it might be out of reach of the smog.

"Let me do the portal; save your energy," Dante instructs as he creates another portal and quickly dials the numbers to our friends.

I don't pay attention to what he's saying or the quiet murmur on the other end. I visibly search the still dark skies for the ends of the polluted air, take a deep breath in, and cough. Even though the air seems clear where we are, there are still particles all around us, too small to see, but our lungs are catching them.

Dante tugs his shirt off and tears it in two, his muscles rippling as he does. A coughing fit rattles him and reminds me of what I did just yesterday. Turning away, all I picture is him on his knees in front of me, choking for air. I massage my palm against my chest in an effort to dull the ache. The invisible threads that connect us are no longer the indestructible cord but now resemble a frayed piece of yarn.

Will we ever be able to get back to what we once were?

"Stay still. This will help," he coaxes, placing the fabric around my face and tying a knot behind my head to create a mask to breathe through. Then, he repeats the process for himself.

It's not perfect, but it'll help. "Thanks."

While I press my hands in again, a groan escapes my lips as I fight to keep the mass contained. I don't want the thickest part spreading past the forest and contaminating the air the people of Graystone need to breathe. Who knows how far it's already traveled? Even with my enhanced sight, the naked eye has its limits.

The ashen cloud rolls in on itself, over and over, until all you see is a charcoal gray ball. Now, what to do with it?

Yuri's prior instructions about floodwater and storm runoff pop into my brain. If I create a hard downpour, I might be able to force the ash back into the volcano. I press the ball in more until it won't compress anymore. Sweat forms along my hairline, and

I grit my teeth. The ash cloud is fighting to break free, and I'm struggling to keep it contained.

Searching the skies I finally find the crater that was left behind. From here, it looks like a vast dark abyss. Continuing to hold the ball of ash, I push my arms straight out, and the mass slowly makes its way over the top of the volcano.

Coughing, I heave another gulp of smoky air into my lungs. Spots dance in my eyes. Concentrating harder, I let go of some of my hold on the gray mass and the skies above darken with clouds heavy with rain. The sound of my own heartbeat pounds in my ears.

It's a delicate balance, loosening my grip on the volcanic plume of smoke just enough for the rain trickling down to push it into that dark crater. My knees wobble and threaten to collapse. A warm body presses up against me from behind as Dante wraps his hands around my stomach.

"I got you. I won't let you fall," Dante says as he rests his head in the crevice between my neck and shoulder.

I close my eyes and revel in the feel of him this close to me. Something cold wraps around my forearm, and my eyes flash open.

Konstantina smiles warmly at me from my right while Reid is on my left. They're both wearing the same bracelets we did during the battle in India when they lent me their strength. They both chant a spell I can't hear over the pulsing in my head. A surge of power flows through my veins, and I double down on the rain. The quicker I force that ash down, the better.

Inch by inch, the ash is removed from the air around us. By the time most of the smog is gone, I'm leaning heavily against Dante's chest. My energy is nearly used up, and I've siphoned a lot from Konstantina and Reid. Releasing my hold on what was once the ash, I spread the rain out farther and farther. Water trickles down around us in a steady stream, and the cool night air sticks to us.

A shiver rolls through my spine, and Dante presses against me harder, trying to shield my body from the cold droplets. Slowly, he backs us away from the edge of the ridge and under the canopy of a tall tree.

The rain continues to fall, and I shift the storm farther away from the volcano and toward civilizations. The rain purifies the air for miles until the clouds shrink and the water ceases to fall. I've met my limit; every bit of magic between us three has been expelled. My head lolls as my vision darkens.

"I'm making a portal to get you all home to rest."

I nod. "Once I can, I want to come back and push the rain out farther."

"We'll come too," Konstantina nods to Reid.

A portal forms in front of us, and Dante twists his body to lift me against his chest before stepping through. Once cleared he cautiously brings me to our bedroom at the castle. Stripping out of my wet clothes, I throw on the ones I wore last night and climb into bed.

Drifting off to sleep, I'm sucked into a dream. My anima gemella sits on a chunk of driftwood, and the waves from the ocean crash on his toes in the sand. He pats the log beside him.

"I thought a change of scenery would be good for both of us," he says quietly. Not meeting my eyes.

The hurt lingers in his voice, and it's like a dagger thrust into my heart. Sitting beside him, I clasp my hands together tightly. My throat burns with the effort of holding back my tears.

"I'm sorry," I whisper.

"I know," Dante answers. "I'm sorry, too."

"For what? You didn't do anything."

He leans into me and puts his arm around my waist.

"That's the problem. I didn't do my job as your mate to protect you."

"You can't protect me from something you can't even see."

"Watch me," he whispers, placing a kiss on my forehead.

Dante

It's been weeks since the situation with Sierra and the volcano erupting. I now only work during her school hours, and she has special permission from Matias to leave school grounds during the week if needed. Sierra finally agreed to see a grief counselor, and I believe it's helping.

Patrolling the streets of Colorado during the day is in stark contrast to the nighttime shift. It's not as busy or dangerous, but it makes the days crawl by at times. Every immortal guardian typically has a rotating schedule, so we're all exposed to every situation. It keeps us sharp. The blacked-out SUV I'm driving chugs along quietly among the humans, blending in.

No matter the time of day, there are always multiple guardians surveying their zones. After we captured Excalibur and imprisoned him, there have been a few incidents in my zone, but nothing huge. Most of the dark ones went on the down low, which doesn't settle well with me. They're planning something big. I can feel it deep in my bones, just like I knew it wasn't over with Excalibur. The Revolution isn't over yet. They're just biding their time. I sigh. I know Sierra is well-protected at the school, but Excalibur has contacts all over. My fear is one of his accomplices will get to her.

I'm on the outskirts of a larger city when my phone buzzes on the dash. Flipping it open and reading the screen, I perk up, hoping to do something other than drive around today.

"Dante speaking," I answer.

"Hey, Dante, what's your location?"

"I'm about a mile out of Whispering Acres."

"I need you to head to Oak Village. It seems there's a werewolf problem."

A werewolf problem? That can mean almost anything.

"Okay. What kind of problem?"

"It's odd. I'm getting reports of them just staging themselves in the park. They're not hurting any humans or anything. Just... there."

"Yeah, that's strange for them. I'm heading that way now," I reply as I pull a U-turn to backtrack to the highway. I'm only about a thirty-minute drive from that town.

I'm curious what their game plan is. "Have you heard anything else?"

"Not a thing. All the chatter from the dark ones has ceased."

That's definitely not a good sign. Maybe I shouldn't have wished for a busier day.

"I'll let you know what I find."

"We'll be in touch. Stay safe out there."

"Will do."

I toss my cell phone in the console and speed up. Once on the highway, I bounce in and out of slower cars until I reach my exit. Rolling the windows down as I come to a stop, no other sounds reach me except for other vehicles. I approach the park Declan directed me to, and the traffic gets heavier. Instead of wasting my time waiting for the line to move, I pull over in a little parking lot. Pocketing my cell phone and slinging my katana over my chest, I'm comforted by the weight of having my most prized weapon with me.

I jog along the sidewalk until I get to a crowd of humans lining the outside of the park. Shouldering through them, I finally glimpse what they're all staring at. At least sixty werewolves in their full wolf form are lining the perimeter of the small grassy park. Massive wolves ranging in shades of browns, grays, blacks, and whites sit there with their heads bowed to the ground, not moving.

I press the button on my earpiece to dial back Declan. "This is Dante requesting backup at Oak Village Park. There are at least sixty wolves on display."

"Back up's on the way, about ten minutes out, and Maverick should be there any time now. I've already looped in the local police for crowd control."

"Thanks."

I slowly walk among the humans, trying to see if the werewolves are circled around something, but the small gaps between the fur don't allow for much. I've never witnessed behavior like this in my years as a guardian. If it weren't for the slow expansion of their chests, they'd resemble statues. The humans are staying about 25 feet away. Sirens echo off in the distance. Hopefully, the boys in blue will cordon off this area. The humans shouldn't be even remotely near this place.

A cold chill racks my body at the thought of what could happen to all of them. Despite the many guardians they're sending to help, I feel severely unprepared. I spot Maverick on the far end of the park on my side and nod.

"What the hell, man? This is eery as shit," his voice reaches me through my earpiece.

"I know, this is a new one."

I waver whether to converse with one of the wolves or wait it out. It's not like I understand wolves. They'd have to change back into a human first. It doesn't look like that will happen soon. It's best to wait until backup arrives and talk to the team about our options.

Local police arrive within minutes. After the confusion of what they see wears off, their training kicks in, and the officers begin ushering the humans back about ten more yards and placing themselves between the humans and the werewolves. My cell phone buzzes in my back pocket, but I don't dare take my eyes off the park.

"This is-"

Whatever name the other immortal guardian was going to say was cut off by the only movement I'd seen inside the park since I came here. They saw it too. A deep silence surrounds us as we all await what will happen. The sounds of multiple cell phones continuing to vibrate sets of alarm bells.

I recognize the werewolf that climbs up the large boulder in the park's center. Koda, the alpha male, is the leader of the entire species. He stands tall enough for the crowd that waits beyond the police to see him. Black tribal designs cover his bare chest and arms.

"This is us taking a stand. We will not be forced to live in the shadows any longer. This is who we are; the humans can either accept sharing this world with us or choose to fight us." He pauses and takes in the crowd beyond us. "A battle they will lose. We choose to live peacefully among humans, but as werewolves, we own the land; we hear the whispers they cannot. We see our prey hiding in the darkness their human eyes can't even comprehend. There's nowhere they can hide where I won't be able to track their scent. If it's a fight they want, it's a fight they'll get. I have long since missed the days of feeling a lesser mortal writhing under me in fright, tasting their blood on my fangs. My fellow lycanthropes, make us known to this world!"

In unison, the werewolves stop bowing their heads and look up at the cloudless sky. A loud, powerful howl resembling a fog horn comes from every wolf, vibrating the ground below us. Koda morphs into his wolf form and joins in with his followers. His shiny black coat, tinged with tiny slivers of white fur, covers an enormous body. He's still perched on the rock as he howls. A strange sensation hits me in the chest through my bond with Sierra.

A hollow silence follows in the aftermath of the howls. The only sound is my heart thudding loudly in my chest. My muscles tense, waiting for them to strike. There are ten other guardians besides Maverick and me surrounding them. That's about a five-to-one ratio, which is not good odds. I know we're good, but that's pushing the limit.

"Dante, what are we doing?" A new voice greets me.

I'm the senior guardian; it's my call to make—still no motion from them. My eyes flick from the alpha to the rest and back again. They know guardians surround them; I've caught glances of them watching us. It seems we're at an impasse. Nobody knows what to expect from the other side. If we attack, we'd be putting us all at a disadvantage, not to mention the humans behind us. I haven't looked in their direction, but I know they're still there.

"We wait," I answer, knowing that with the werewolves' keen hearing, they can also hear our voices.

Another few minutes go by before Koda's body starts to fold in on itself, changing back into a man. Once entirely morphed, he slowly walks in my direction. His gaze sweeps across the crowd and the rest of my team, but ultimately, his yellow irises land on me. Every nerve ending's on fire, and every muscle is tensing, preparing to defend. Out of my peripheral vision, my team does the same. Slowly, my hand reaches up to my katana to rest on its hilt. My palm itches to bring her out of the wooden scabbard that protects the blade.

"No need for that. I don't want any trouble. Dante, I presume?" Koda stops a few feet in front of me.

I'm not a little guy by any means. Standing next to him, though, I feel small. He stands several inches taller, and his shoulders are broader than mine. The large biceps and forearms match the rest of his buff build. I lower my arm but not my guard. I don't know what he wants.

"Yes, I'm Dante." My hand rests on the belt around my waist just above my dagger.

"I'm Koda, the Alpha of all Alphas." At this, he reaches his hand out for me to shake, and I take his firm grip.

"You do what you must, but just know my men are prepared to defend. We won't go quietly. Tell me, Dante, how much is your guardian oath worth to you? Is it worth losing everything for? The dark ones are rising up. There aren't enough guardians to keep us down. Will you stand with us to abolish this injustice or rally against us?"

I look to Maverick, who stands beside me, and the men that dot the park's edges. Equal parts want me to strike and stand my ground or stand beside the alpha and fight for their rights. A war rages on inside me. This could mean an all-out war from all sides.

"What will you choose guardian?"

A sharp pain lances through my body, stemming from the amulet around my neck. I clutch at my stomach; the pain is nearly unbearable. My knees wobble below me, and saliva pools in my mouth. Something's happened to Sierra.

"I choose Sierra," I choke out. "It'll always be her."

Tugging the blue benitoite stone from my pocket, I create a portal to Sierra and jump through before it's even fully formed.

Chapter 18

Sierra

Alarms start to blare on the loudspeaker above me. A loud booming voice from Headmaster Matias comes on, "This is not a drill. The academy is on full lockdown. Lock the doors and do exactly as your professors tell you. Until I say otherwise, use any means necessary to protect the lives of those around you. You may be young, but this is what you're training for. We fight!"

My eyes dart to my other classmates who share a similar shocked face to our instructor, Audrey. What the hell is going on? We've had practice drills, but nothing like this. A loud noise like snow coming off the roof thunders around us, and the girls behind me scream.

"It's okay! It's just the security shutters coming down. Get to the weapons closet, now," she barks the command.

All the students immediately scramble over to the small room that holds numerous weapons. My hands tremble slightly as I reach for a set of daggers that resemble my own back at the cabin. Students aren't allowed to have their own on the academy's grounds. Tucking the knives into the belt slung around my waist, I try to swallow down the panic.

This can't be real. It's just another drill, one made to simulate reality. My breaths come in shallow pants as the walls close in around me, bringing me back to when I was on that battlefield.

Cell phones ding, and I reach for mine in my back pocket. It's Emma asking if I'm alright. I text her back quickly before silencing the ringer.

"Everybody grab the weapon that's most comfortable for you." Then, more quietly, she says, "Sierra, come here."

As I reach her, she holds her hands out for mine. Not understanding what she wants, I go to grasp her hand, but she unclasps the iron bracelet around my wrist. I begin to pull my arm back and tell her, "I have to keep these on; Matias said if I-"

"Sierra, he said by any means necessary. You and I both know that your gift is more of a weapon than anything these students can wield."

"I don't think I can do this again." I hate the slight tremble in my voice. I loathe how I feel like that helpless girl I was back on the plane. I vowed to be better, to be stronger.

"Look at me. You and I are the only ones in this room that have seen actual combat. All these students are relying on us to lead them." She shakes my shoulders. "You and I, we got this, okay?" Her eyes bore into me, and her grip tightens around my forearms.

I cast another glance at the others. What used to be fear of me clouding their vision is now acceptance.

Nodding, I say, "Okay."

A loud explosion rattles the building, and screams erupt not far from us. My breathing becomes shallow again, and my palms begin to sweat. All I can think of is Emma. I rack my brain, trying to remember where her class is right now. Everything is so scattered I can't remember anything straight. Thoughts of Excalibur take over every rational thought. I'm right back to the last time an explosion rocked my world. My vision darkens before I scrub both hands over my face to wipe the images away.

Tugging out my phone again, I text both Emma and Dante; I only hear back from Emma that she's safe—no word from Dante. I slow my breathing and try to reach out to him through our bond. I'm not as in tune as he is. I'm only getting a vague feeling of wariness. Maybe he already knows what's happening and is too busy helping to reply.

My phone vibrates, and I yank it out. My eyebrows scrunch together, and I frown. Nilo? He hardly ever contacts me, and he's calling over video chat.

"Hello?" I answer with a scratchy voice.

"Sierra, thank the ancestors. You need to listen to me right now." His face is pinched, and his eyes are crinkled at the edges with worry. The background is nothing but a blur, so he must be running.

"We're under attack. The academy's on lockdown, there was an explosion-"

"I know. They're coming for you, Sierra."

The breath halts from my lungs, and the blood in my veins turns to ice. The surrounding chaos of the student's panicked voices ceases to exist. His words, "They're coming for you, Sierra," rattles around in my brain.

"What, why?" I'm surprised I could string those two words together.

"They're targeting the keys... Willow's dead." He pauses and swallows hard, turning away from the screen. "Konstantina and Reid are missing. Teiresias saw it right before it happened and tried to warn them. He's in hiding, but none of us are safe."

No. Not Willow. An ache sets inside my chest, and my blood begins to boil in anger.

"What do I do?" I clutch at the small leather pouch hidden under my shirt and squeeze. This is what they're after.

"You unleash the wrath of the deities on anyone who tries to harm you, no matter who they are. It was Maggie who attacked Willow; she's been working with Excalibur all along. Trust nobody. The fate of the world rests on our survival."

My jaw clenches—that witch. I knew there was something more to her than just my jealousy flaring when she flirted with Dante. I freaking knew it! I should've trusted my gut. If I had, Willow might still be alive.

"But what about the others here? They're all in danger." So many innocent lives are here at the school. My stomach lurches. Oh my god, the younger kids are in the other building.

I pray to every deity above that they protect them. They're completely innocent and helpless. They can't even defend themselves yet.

"No war doesn't have casualties. Save who you can, but the most important life you need to protect is yours. If Excalibur gets free, it will quite literally be hell on earth. And everybody's lives will be in jeopardy. Stay strong, and until we can figure out how to get it under control, stay safe."

"You too." I click the button to hang up. I'm not really processing everything he just said. I tilt my head up to find Audrey's wide eyes watching me.

I go to speak, but she quickly interjects, "I heard."

Another loud boom echoes from across the academy's grounds. "Are they bombing the school?"

"I'm afraid so," she says.

"Then we're just sitting ducks here. We should leave."

"And if we go out there without the cover of the building, they'll spot us immediately. And take us out easier." She glances all around the classroom as if looking for an escape.

A frustrated growl escapes my throat. I can't sit here and let innocent people die because of me. "If it's me they want, then I'll leave. Everybody will be safer."

"No," Audrey snaps. "We stand together. Immortal guardians fight their battles *together*. If your life is what keeps him imprisoned, we won't let you die. Who's with me?" She turns to the others, who have been eerily silent.

"We are!" The shouts from the other students startle me. I didn't even realize they heard our conversation. And I'm flabbergasted that they would even stand beside me. I thought they hated me, feared me, and didn't even want me here.

"Okay, here's what we're going to do; we're bringing the fight to them. What exactly can you do with your gift?"

After filling her in, she types away on her cell phone before jabbing it in her back pocket. She calmly opens the classroom door a few inches and pokes her head out.

"We're good," Audrey says before opening it all the way.

Single file, we tiptoe out into the vast hall. There's been no other announcements over the intercom. We're going in blind and don't know where the insurgents are. The smell of something burning scents the air. Slowly, we creep to the backside of the structure. That's where the explosions came from. We round the last corner, and smoke billows from the wreckage of a large hole in the wall. Calling on my element, I douse the flames and crawl through the rubble. The stones are scalding beneath my palms, and steam rises. The rock my foot is on crumples, and my foot slips.

"Be careful," Audrey whispers.

Once I'm through the small opening, I hear shouts outside. Glancing around, I see nothing but debris littering the back lawn. Sunlight dances off the shiny metal shutters that came down to protect the building. I don't see anybody.

"Where are they?" I ask.

"I don't know; try to stick to the shadows and spread out. Have your weapons ready," Audrey urges.

Coming to the corner of the building, I peek around the edge, and my stomach drops. It's just like India. A range of dark ones and guardians are fighting. Some are already dead on the ground. I quickly look away; I can't see that right now. I need to focus on the living. Sucking a huge breath in, I let it out and center my thoughts before exposing myself.

A vampire stands at the edge of the woods, unable to enter the lawn under the full sun. There must be close to thirty others that lurk in the dense trees. If I cause a thunderstorm, that can darken the skies enough to allow them out in the open.

Her sharp eyes find mine, and she flashes her fangs. "Just give us the Immortal Savior, and we'll leave."

"We do not bow to your kind," a male professor snarls before slamming his stake into her heart.

The vampire lets out a hiss, but I don't have time to watch what happens as a low, menacing growl shakes the ground.

A water bomb forms in my hand before I thrust it at him. It only manages to knock him off balance. Another werewolf emerges to my left as Audrey lunges to attack it. Lightning cracks the sky, and the hairy beast falls to the ground. I'm flung backward as a heavy mass of hair crushes me to the ground. My hands instinctually grab the werewolf's neck as his teeth clap together, aiming for my throat. His yellow eyes are terrifying up close, and I cringe as his hot breath gets closer.

Think! What the hell am I supposed to do? I can't make a storm or do lightning this close to me, or I'll fry myself and him. My arms shake from the force of keeping his massive jaw from closing on me. I try to pull the water from him like I have others, but I can't. Not when I'm fighting his body so hard. I can't focus my mind enough to create ice bullets, either. His teeth graze my shoulder and tear away at my flesh. I cry out as I hear others fighting similar battles close to me. The bite stings as if acid's been poured over it.

Frost begins to cover my hands as I stretch out my fingers until they resemble long claw-like icicles that wrap around his dark gray fur. Angling my thumbs toward his throat, a string of saliva slaps at my face as his powerful jaws keep snapping closer and closer to me. A yell escapes me as his wiry fur touches the skin on my cheek. He's getting too close.

"Get off me!" I scream.

Talons jut out from my fingers, piercing the werewolf's throat from all ten of my fingers. Hot burgundy blood drips down my hands and arms as I watch the life drain from his eyes. I shove his heavy body off me, and it thuds against the hard ground.

I find Alessia in a similar position. Bolting toward her, I vault onto the beast's back and spear my fingers into his chest. While he thrashes beneath me, the ice breaks off from my fingers, but he's still alive. At least his focus is on me now, not Alessia, who's staring in shock and is no help to me. Sliding the dagger from its sheath at my side, I plunge it deep into his chest cavity as he lunges for me. One final howl escapes from his massive body.

"The rules have changed; the attack on the academy is to find the person with the key to setting Excalibur free. We need to fight together to stop them from getting to her. We are the guardians of Graystone, and they're threatening our home, our people," Matias's voice echoes across the land.

I scan the crowd, trying to figure out who the good guys are and who the bad are. Nilo's command comes back, "Trust nobody."

Who could do this? Screams and shouts come from inside the academy's walls. Emma! They must be inside. My thoughts scatter as I try to focus on what needs to be done. I can't run in there just for Emma. They all need me. "She's safe," I whisper to myself. I'd know if she were hurt.

As I turn away, my foot snags on a body, and I nearly topple on top of them. The blood drains from my face.

"No." It's Jack.

His blue eyes stare straight up at me, dull and lifeless. My eyes water and blur his features. I check his pulse, knowing full well he's already gone. There's no heartbeat. With two fingers, I gently close his eyelids. "Your death won't be in vain. They'll pay for this," I promise through gritted teeth.

As I straighten, my gaze lands on the silver sword that lies beside him. Fresh blood still coats the blade. He died fighting. I glance at the building my best friend may be in. I won't let them win.

A thought occurs to me, one that Yuri commanded me. "Why dance in the rain when I can bring the storm?"

I am the storm!

Chapter 19

Sierra

Lifting the sword, it begins to glow pink and white as little streaks of lighting shift around the blade like molten metal. The sword becomes almost weightless as I swing it toward the werewolf, who lunges at me with a wide-open jaw. The blade slices clean through his throat, ending his assault.

Another scream comes from the wood line. Far too many vampires wait for me to make the storm they no doubt assumed I'd do right off. I won't give them that advantage unless I absolutely have to. There are already too many enemies circling us.

"Is that a fucking dragon?" Adeline screeches behind me.

My head snaps in the other direction, and my stomach plummets. Because, indeed, there is a large dragon flapping its massive wings in the sky and barreling toward us. A nearly deafening roar comes from the large black and red creature as a blast of fire shoots from his mouth.

I stare up at it with equal parts awe and terror. I stand there watching even though everything in me tells me to run. To get as far away from that dragon as I can.

Of course, it could be any dragon, and yet it had to be a damn fire-breathing one? I sheath my sword at my side and plant my feet. Closing my eyes, I feel the water source thrumming through me, giving me energy. Thrusting my open palm toward the scaly beast, several bolts of lightning flow from my skin and strike the dragon.

He cries out in agony, and for a brief few seconds, his wings stop flapping, and it begins to fall from the sky faster and faster until his body convulses and begins rapidly pushing the air beneath him. Then he sets his attention on me.

"Run!" I scream at the group that formed behind me. "Get to the younger students building!"

We're stuck halfway between the buildings, fighting off the army that I'm assuming Excalibur sent to kill me. I can't watch any more people die at his hands, whether he's here or not. This is his doing. He won't kill innocent children on my watch. Hell no. If he taught me anything in those mind games of dreams, it's that we can never rest and think we're safe.

No. Because there's always a monster ready to attack. It was all our fault for thinking we were safe at the academy.

The other students run toward the stone building that houses the young, but Audrey remains at my side. I nod toward the building. "Go, Audrey."

"I'm not going anywhere. They attack my school, my students? I would rather die fighting than live my life cowering behind others. This is what a guardian does. This is what we're meant for."

"Okay, stay close. I can try to shield us in a bubble so the dragon's fire won't come through." I press my hands out to my sides, and a wall of water forms from the ground in a backward waterfall, up and over us, flowing back into the grass. A constant stream of liquid circles around us as another explosion rocks the ground beneath us.

"Why aren't they evacuating?" I ask as I squeeze my hands together and pull them out slowly.

Even though it may allow the vampires to advance, I have no other option. Plenty of immortal guardians are flanking the school, trained to fight off the dark ones. A menacing cloud begins to take shape in the sky, and I wave my hand around in a circle, creating hurricane-force winds that blow our enemies back several feet, giving me a moment to think.

I spot several professors making their way through the throng of demons that spawned on the right side of the field. Clanging swords and shouts reach my ears even over the howling wind whipping around us.

"If we can make it to them, we could spread out and surround the school from this side. We could keep them away from the young." Audrey suggests.

"If they're close to me, that automatically makes them more of a target."

"Sierra, you may be new to Graystone, but this is what we stand for. Unity. You are one of us, even if you don't yet bear the mark of a guardian. It's an honor to fight beside you." She closes her fist and thumps her chest in a show of respect.

I copy the movement; my throat tightens painfully, knowing that somebody outside my small circle of friends will fight with me. She reminds me so much of my mother my chest aches. Is this what my mom was like in battle?

Another deafening roar as the dragon speeds toward us, faster and faster. His wings flap until they move so fast it's like a blur.

"What do I do?" I ask Audrey. "How do you kill a dragon?" I hold the shield in place as flames shoot out from its mouth—my arms spasm underneath the tension.

"I don't know. I never knew there were dragons!" Audrey shouts as the powerful blast of fire, fights to break through my shield.

Pressing my arms out, I groan under the pressure. It's like there's a forcefield around his flames pushing harder and harder to get through. The flames stop as he turns quickly and takes off toward the clouds. I watch as he circles high above the trees.

"Maybe he needs time to recharge between trying to roast us?" Audrey suggests. "Let's get closer to the others."

Dropping my shield so I can recharge my powers, the water crashes to the ground. We run across the grounds, which separates us from the other teachers and guardians. Audrey's blade slices through the arm of a man running toward us.

Screaming in agony, he drops to the ground, and we rush closer to the group standing guard in front of the large building that holds the youngest immortal children.

Scanning the field before me, I'm brought back to that terrible night we attacked Excalibur's fort. My eyes dart from body to body; some are still standing, and several are lying in a heap. I'm desperately trying to spot my best friend. The breath seizes in my lungs when my gaze drifts over a small body with long blonde hair. I can't help it; I dash to her and brush the hair off her face.

It's not Emma. I don't recognize her, but she's no longer breathing. I gently pull her lids down over her light green eyes. "Rest in peace."

"Come on, we have to move. The best way to help them is to take these bastards down."

Nodding, I stand and continue sprinting across the grass.

"The wards are up; nothing's getting through to them now," Matias's booming voice is heard.

At least the rest of the academy is safe.

"It's coming back," somebody shouts down the line.

I fling my hands up, and the water rises in front of us, flowing over our heads and back down to the ground.

"Matias!" I yell. "How do we kill it?"

His face tells me everything he didn't have to say. Not even he knows how to kill a dragon.

Is this just another thing that the High Council hid from its people? There has to be a way. Everything has a weakness. I can't hold him off forever. My magic will be drained soon without having a witch to siphon from.

He barrels ever closer, and another roar bellows from him. This one is so loud my chest feels the rumble. My breaths quicken as I brace for impact and push with all my might as the shield quakes under his assault.

"Audrey," I say as a wave of dizziness rushes through my veins.

"I'm right here." She rests her hand on my shoulder to steady me.

"I can't shield everyone." My throat constricts. "They need to go."

Again, the beast bolts higher into the air. But he won't be gone for long.

"What if we create a diversion?" Yuri speaks up.

"What do you mean?" Matias asks.

"The rest of the guardians and staff can break off onto the east side. It's after Sierra, so we use her as bait."

My spine goes rigid. The words Nilo said, "Don't trust anyone," ring in my head. Yuri helped me so much these past few months. I know I've been gullible before, but I highly doubt she intends to hurt me.

"And how do you suppose we do that?" Audrey snaps.

"Sierra can create that bubble around herself, but meanwhile, it's actually me that's within it. Cloning magic, if you will."

My mind races. "And then what?"

"When the beast attacks, we portal below and attack them in the soft spot of their abdomen."

"How do you know that's the weakness?" Matias asks.

"That's where most beings' weakness lies. It also angles its stomach away from us anytime it comes close."

"That could work. But I think we'll only have one shot. The likelihood of the dragon falling for it a second time is slim," Matias admits.

"And then comes the issue of our blades; I don't think they'll be able to get past the thick scales of armor. But Sierra's, with her magic, might be able to penetrate it," Yuri adds.

Audrey bristles. "There's an awful lot of coulds, mights, and possibly's in that plan."

"I don't know what our other options are."

"I'll do it." My blade comes alive, the lightning licking all the way up to the hilt as I balance the weight. "I won't be able to hold the shield and enchant my sword, though."

"I understand."

My eyes meet Yuri's. "I won't be able to keep the fire off you. I'll try, but I don't think I can do both."

"I'm aware of the risk. The dragon's turning back now. Create a shield nobody can see through. I'll clone you, and then you need to portal right where his stomach will be."

The rest of the professors disperse, except Matias and Audrey.

"Are you sure about this, Yuri?" Matias steps closer.

"I am, sir. Let's slay this beast."

He thumps his fist against his chest, and we do the same, knowing full well that Yuri most likely won't make it out of this. Bringing the shield back up, I turn to Audrey.

"I'll create the portal. You'll go through it first, and then we'll go through it, okay?" Audrey asks.

I nod as bile rises in my throat.

"Ready?"

"Yup."

The dragon roars as he nears, and the fire blasts the ground leading up to us. The grasses catch on fire and spread. A portal opens, and I leap through simultaneously, forcing my gift into my sword. Lightning dances up the razor-sharp length, and I shove up above me as brutal and swift as I can muster. The blade plunges into the beast's chest while I blast my magic with all my might into him. My hands graze the smooth scales of armor that cover its body as my weapon reaches the hilt, and the dragon shrieks painfully loud.

Lightning cracks across the sky in a blinding light, sending me backward. My body hits the side of the stone building with a sickening sound, instantly making me dizzy and nauseous. A portal opens up beside me, and Dante steps through. He must've felt it through our bond that things were going really, really bad.

Concern is etched into every frown line on his handsome face. His green eyes are shrouded in anger as he takes in the scene. I try to get up to go to him, but I can't move. Everything feels tingly and shattered at the same time. The bubble I created begins to come crashing to the ground like a rogue wave.

But I was able to save Yuri. She's still standing.

Behind Dante, several more guardians pile through and join the line. More portals open up across the vast openness, and guardians continue to spill out of them. Pulling at my gift again to try to rebuild the wall, I only manage to gain a few inches of height before it crashes back down. The dragon is lying on the ground several yards from me.

I try to build a shield around the dragon with everything I have, but still, it's not enough. My hand falls to my stomach, and it lands in something wet. Pulling my hand up, I see it's coated in crimson-colored blood.

My eyes meet Dante's before looking down at my belly. Blood soaks through my t-shirt, and a large gash is sliced nearly from one side to the other. It must've happened when I stabbed the dragon. He must've shoved me away with his claws, which flung me back.

Dante's katana clatters to the ground, and he drops to his knees in front of me. "I need a healer!" his strangled plea rings out through the chaos.

He sits beside me on the now bloodied ground, tearing his shirt off; he wads it into a tight ball and presses it against my wound. I hiss in pain. Crap, that hurts; I squeeze my eyes shut as spots dance in my vision. Dante gently presses his lips against my forehead, and a sense of peace starts to come over me. I relax against the cool stone behind me. My eyelids grow heavy as if sandbags are weighing them down.

"Sierra, don't you dare die on me. You hear me?" his voice trembles. "Healer!" he shouts again, this time so forceful I can feel it rumble through my chest.

Lifting my hand, I cup his stubbled chin and try to memorize every last detail of his face, from his dark, chocolatey brown hair, emerald green eyes, and sharp jawline. He's still applying pressure on my stomach, but it's a dull ache at this point. I'm not naïve; I understand the meaning of that—tears well beneath my heavy lids. I didn't think I'd have to say goodbye already. My heart shatters.

"I love you, Dante," I whisper.

"Do not say your goodbyes. You're not going anywhere."

This really is the end for me. I feel everything slipping away as if running my hand through the water.

"Please." I cough, and blood splatters on my hand as I cover my mouth. "I just need to hear you say it."

He swallows thickly as he gazes down at me with so much love and anguish in those beautiful green eyes. Wetness coats them, and a few tears leak out and fall onto my cheeks. "I love you, my beautiful north star, more than anything in this world or the next. But I swear to all the deities, if you die," his voice cracks. "I will unleash a hell like they've never seen before. They should've protected you!"

"Move your hands, Dante," a higher-pitched voice appears beside us. Yuri I think.

Dante's eyes flick to the side, but I don't look away from his face. The pressure eases on my middle, and more blood trickles down my sides before Yuri places her bare hands directly onto my skin. I cough up more blood and struggle to rake in a breath.

Dante cradles my head in his hands and places a feather-light kiss on my lips. His forehead meets mine, and we share each other's breaths. Heat radiates out from the hands on my stomach. A burning sensation tears across my skin like a blistering sunburn. I bite down on my lip to keep from crying out at the pain.

"Helios needs you to survive. I need you to survive. You can do this: fight the darkness, Sierra. You fight it," he barks the command out. His warm breath fans my face like a caress. "Remember what you told our son? You'd fight Satan himself; you'd move heaven and hell for him. This is not how our story ends."

Helios and Dante are my last thoughts as darkness swoops in and everything else disappears. No sounds. No lights. No feelings. Just empty, eerie darkness as the thudding of my heart slows to match the blood trickling out of me.

The end for now... The Rise Of Chaos is coming soon!

I want to thank my husband and kids, first of all, without their support, there literally would be no books... I spend countless hours working a "real job" to come home and spend more hours writing, editing, marketing and engaging with readers. Writing has always been a dream of mine and if it weren't for them I wouldn't be able to do it all.

A huge shout-out goes out to my ARC team, old and new, who have stuck by me through my most recent book or have been with me since the first one. I love hearing how much my stories have affected you and I'm thankful you're on this rollercoaster ride with me! Having such an amazing team to help get the word out about my books is a massive help.

For my readers, thank you for taking a chance on a newer author like myself. I truly hope you enjoyed reading the third installment of the Destiny Of Graystone series and it would mean so much to me if you could share your review of Thorn Of Darkness on Goodreads and the retailer website!

Katie lives on the east coast with her husband and their children. When she's not working or spending time with her family, she enjoys getting lost in a good book. Her favorite hobby is gardening, whether it is edible or decorative. In her opinion one can never have too many flowers! She may have a slight addiction to creating things in Canva and Procreate. Visit https://www.katierichard.com for more information and to sign up for her newsletter. The QR code below brings you to all of Katie's links!

9 7 9 8 9 8 8 7 4 8 6 9 4